WOLF'S INSTINCT

ELVA BIRCH

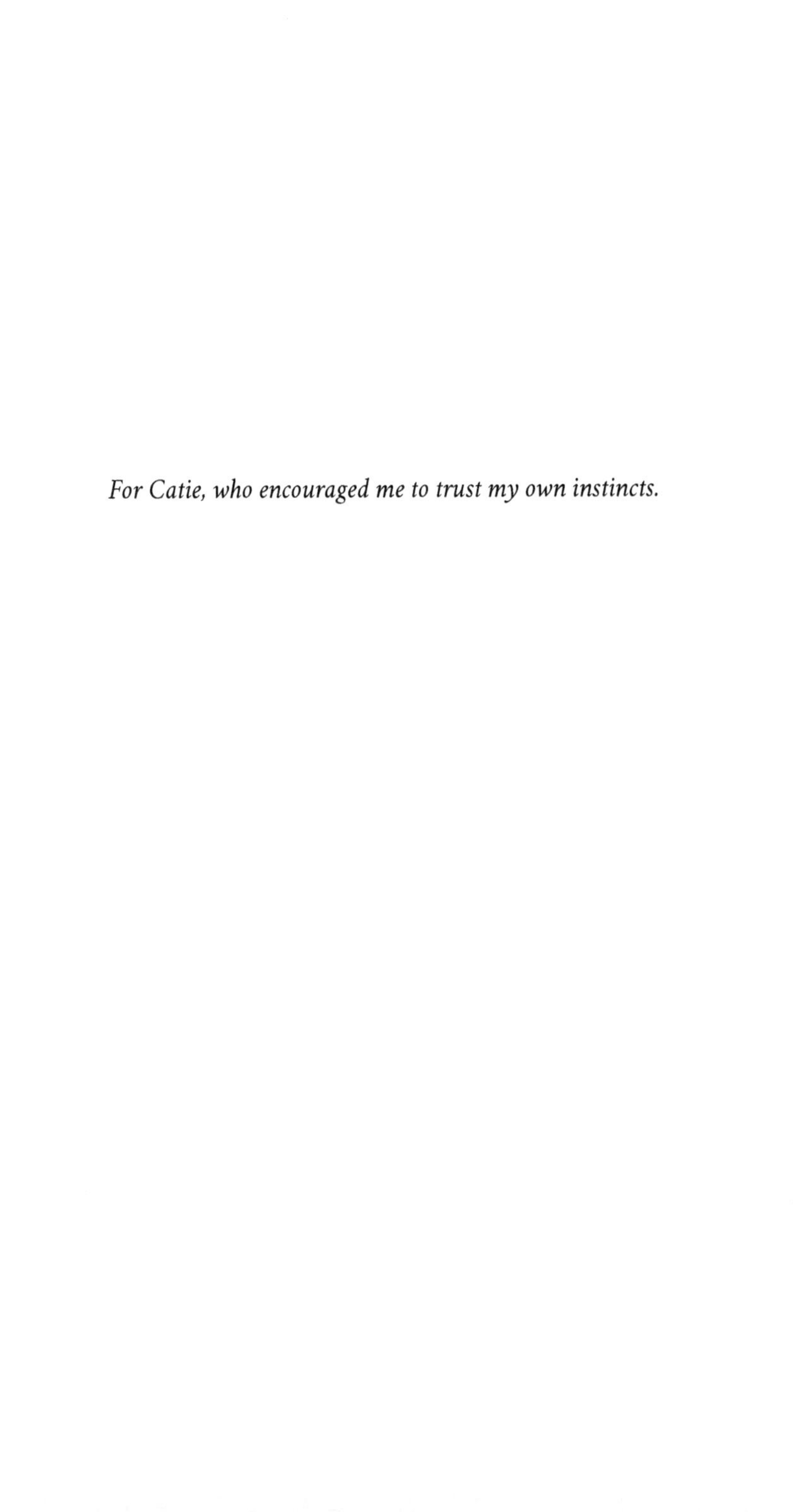

For Catie, who encouraged me to trust my own instincts.

1

Don't swear in front of the kids, don't swear in front of the kids, don't swear... Roderick wrenched his shoulder nearly out of the socket trying to reach through the tiny hole under the sink to get to the fitting. Inside his head was a far less censored litany.

"Uck!"

Had he said it out loud after all?

"Uck! Uck!"

Roderick craned his head around and saw a little girl with a blond halo of fuzzy hair standing in the door. She looked about the age of his own daughter, Gabby, but was standing confidently on both feet, a spit-soggy stuffed animal in one hand.

A spry middle-aged woman with salt-and-pepper and electric-blue pigtails swooped in behind her and lifted the child out of the way of the spreading puddle of dirty water leaking from beneath the sink.

"How did you get past the table?" Cherry demanded cheerfully of the child. Her wild-colored hair was at odds with her conservative country plaid shirt and plain jeans.

Her feet were in socks, and she was careful to stay clear of the mess.

"Uck!" the toddler replied merrily.

Roderick looked sheepishly at Cherry.

"Yuck," Cherry agreed. "Yuck is right!"

Oh, yuck. Yuck was okay, even if it wasn't at all what Roderick had been thinking.

"What's the news?" Cherry asked, lowering her voice.

"Not good," Roderick said, shaking his head. He'd finally gotten his fingers around the fitting and could unscrew it and draw it out of the tiny access panel in the wet wall. "Whoever plumbed this building ought to be…" he glanced at the little girl chortling in Cherry's arm. "Yuck," he said. "Let's just go with yuck."

He wriggled out from under the sink and inspected the fitting. "I really should take a look at the rest of them, too. If they put these everywhere, you could have a big problem on your hands."

Cherry peered at the fitting. "What's wrong with it?"

"Besides the fact that this is a totally inappropriate fitting for this spot, it's the wrong material. Not to code for potable water."

"Is it toxic?" Cherry asked in horror, exchanging a look with the child in her arms.

"Uck!" the little girl added, trying to squirm free and play in the water on the floor.

"It's relatively harmless," Roderick promised. "But it should all be replaced if this isn't the only one. This stuff tends to wear out faster, especially if it goes through a lot of temperature changes. It also looks like maybe the system was frozen with water in it." He pointed out a crack in the fitting. "There may be other cracks."

"The place was empty last winter," Cherry said, looking around in despair. "Maybe it wasn't winterized first?"

"I hope you're not having second thoughts about expanding your day care business," Roderick said.

"No," Cherry said firmly, and she gave him a genuine smile. "I'm excited about it. I just dread explaining to Veronica that she's going to have to spend money on the place."

"It's a great place," Roderick agreed.

Cherry's scowl spread effortlessly to an excited grin. "I love it already," she said frankly.

Cherry had been babysitting for Roderick and other shifters in Nickel City for decades, and he'd watched the demand for her services outgrow her house and her ability to watch them all on her own. She'd decided to make the leap to opening a day care downtown and hire a helper or two.

Roderick had been the one to find the place, despite his reservations about the landlord, and was sorry that her opening day had been met with a bathroom flood; he wished that he had better news for her.

The girl in her arms fussed and then seamlessly shifted into a fuzzy little owl chick, beating downy wings in protest of her captivity as she wiggled from her clothes.

"Whoops," Cherry said, easily tossing her in place as she gathered up the clothing. "Clever little Amy, but you still can't play in this mess, even as an owl! I gotta go check on the other kids. My new hire should be here in just a few minutes."

Roderick was surprised by a jangle at the fringes of his wolf's senses. Why would his shifter instinct be excited by *that* news? Sometimes he felt like instinct was a game of hot-and-cold with a kid who had forgotten where they'd hid something, with no hint of logic or direction. He'd learned to treat it with a degree of reserve—since a simple *that way* could lead him right off the edge of a cliff—but never to ignore it.

"Who did you get?" he asked, grabbing the mop to clean up the mess.

"Wendy—you know Wendy from the DMV? Her cousin from Buffalo was looking for work. I haven't even met her yet," Cherry confessed, "but her resume was impressive. She has a certificate in early education, and she worked as a nanny for a shifter family who gave her a glowing recommendation. Wendy said she'd suit me and, well, it's not like I have a lot of choices."

Hiring reliable help for a day care was hard enough. Hiring help for a day care for shifters? That could get complicated. Not only did they have to be part of a secret community, but they still had to meet all the usual human-world qualifications and pass background checks. Maybe his instinct was just confirming that Cherry had picked a good candidate. After all, whoever she was, his daughter would be spending time in her care, so she definitely mattered to his little family of two.

"I'm going to get my ladder and check out the other fittings in the ceiling," Roderick told Cherry. "I'll let you know what I find."

Why would his instinct insist that he was about to find happiness?

2

The only thing "city" about Nickel City was its name, Addison decided.

Her first day in the little town, she drove to visit several of the historical locations featured in the glossy brochure that her cousin Wendy provided for her. There were some quaint mining displays and a few interpretive signs about the brief prospecting rush that had built the town when stainless steel drove up demand for the mineral nickel. An entire bustling museum was devoted to nickels, boasting the most comprehensive collection of three-cent and wooden nickels in the United States. It had one of those commemorative coin-squishing machines out front and several laughing boys were putting it through its paces.

Each of the numbered destinations was more crowded than she expected them to be, with people who were obviously tourists snapping photos on their phones and dragging bored children behind them. There was a slightly surly feeling to the locals serving them, and Addison was surprised and a little delighted to run across not just one but two other shifters in her little self-guided tour, each of them giving her a little tingle of awareness at the edges of her nerves when they were close by.

They each exchanged a little smile and nod of recognition, but nothing more.

Nickel City had a busy little downtown with familiar coffee shop chains and fast food, but the office buildings didn't top four stories at the most, and the only box store was ten miles out of town. The little town seemed to be more trees than buildings, and indeed, a sign in town proudly pronounced it a member of "Tree City, USA."

In fact, one of the town's claims to fame was a particularly spectacular larch on a private estate near Belle Lake with a plaque declaring the fragrant pine the third-largest tree in all of Montana. It was open to visitors on each second and fourth Thursday, and Addison was surprised to realize that her timing was that perfect.

She visited it to satisfy her inner lynx's characteristic feline curiosity and wasn't sure what to make of the shiver of recognition that ran through her at the sight of it. It wasn't threatening, and it wasn't welcoming, simply weirdly aware. She reached inward, asking a question wordlessly, and her lynx gave an unconcerned feline shrug. Maybe any tree that old was slightly magic and it wasn't instinct at all.

A little older woman with fluffy gray hair and a bright red shirt stood beside her in the crowd, giving Addison's senses a not-quite-shifter tickle. "It's something, isn't it?" the stranger said proudly.

They stood a little apart from the other tourists, who were trying to take photos and selfies, complaining that you couldn't really see the scope of the tree in their pictures.

"I've never seen anything like it," Addison admitted. She didn't even try to photograph it, knowing that no snapshot could capture the sheer size and power of the thing. There was no way to even see the top.

"It's one hundred and seventy feet tall," the woman told her. "And the crown is thirty-five feet in diameter. It's almost a thousand years old."

She didn't look like a tourist, Addison decided. She didn't have a backpack or camera or even a purse. She was wearing something like a vintage pin-up girl, straight out of a World War II photo shoot. Did trees have docents like museums did?

Some of the tourists were circling the tree to show that four of them together could barely reach around the broad trunk, their friend taking shots on her phone. One of them gave a cry of disgust. "There's sap on me! Oh, gross, it's sticky!"

"That's what she said!" one of his friends chortled.

Addison giggled and glanced at the woman beside her to see how she'd take the joke and found that she had vanished. She looked around curiously but didn't see the woman's distinctive red blouse anywhere in the thin crowds.

* * *

The following day, Addison found her new place of employment.

Potential employment, she reminded herself, looking up at the false storefront with a smile of amusement and excitement.

A block off of the main street, this area had clearly been made to imitate a gold rush town, with a quaint fake second story all along the street. She doubted that it was actually a historic district, but suspected that it was something more recent, to capitalize on the town's mining history, even though its real resource had been nickel and not gold, and the big rush had been in the 1950s and 60s, not in the 1800s. It was a curious mix of rustic and modern, with rough wood siding and chrome fixtures side by side. Addison suspected it would give an actual historian apoplectic fits.

She knew she was at the right place; a large sign above the door declared "Saloon" in an old-fashioned font. The windows to either side were obscured with colorful tissue paper in a bright, bold geometric pattern, allowing sunlight in, but not prying eyes. Instinct was humming in her veins, promising...Addison wasn't sure what, but she had to squash the feeling that she was exactly when and where she was supposed to be. Whatever instinct was good for, it could swamp her ability to speak logically, and she was here for an interview and wanted all her wits sharp and her mind clear.

The door was locked and there was a doorbell with a speaker and the gleam of a camera right next to it, with a cheerful note that said, "Ring for Cherry!"

Addison drew in a breath and pressed the button briefly.

There was a static crackle of something that might have been Cherry's name, almost drowned by a child's shriek.

Addison depressed the intercom button again and said into the box, "This is Addison Carmichael," as clearly as she could.

The answer was completely garbled, but there was a little buzz and click at the door. Addison opened it cautiously and walked into an entryway fenced by walls that didn't quite reach the wood-paneled ceiling. She could hear laughter and children's voices beyond the divider, as well as the yelp of a puppy.

A poster of a bear wiggling weirdly human toes was the first thing that greeted Addison, with stencil letters that said: "'BEAR' FEET PLEASE. SHOES OFF." Beneath that was a handwritten note that said, "Please put socks in shoes if you are not going to wear them so they don't get lost."

There were two tiny, unmatched socks pinned up next to it.

Under the windows on each side of the door ran two low, unpadded benches, and facing each of them was a row of hooks. Half a dozen of them had bags and jackets hanging at them, and there were several pairs of shoes tucked under the bench.

Addison sat down at the bench and took off her tennis shoes, tucking them underneath neatly and pairing up the chaos of toddler shoes she found there out of general habit.

At the end of the hooks to the left was a doorway arch through the partial wall, blocked by a baby gate.

Standing guard at the gate was a toddler, a little older than a year, clinging to the molded plastic for balance as she bounced happily in place. Black curly hair crowned her head, and she wore a green romper covered in frogs. She had clearly just discovered that she had knees and was testing them exuberantly.

"Gaba!" she announced when Addison approached and peered cautiously past her. "Gaba!"

There was a room divider, so that she had to step carefully over the gate and the toddler and take several steps before she could see into the room itself.

Inside was delightful pandemonium.

A big-pawed, mixed-breed puppy was tussling with a growling bear cub and a tiny, curled-up armadillo rocked under their feet, barely escaping from being trampled in the play. A gawky baby owl, not fledged yet, was bouncing in place, beating its fluffy wings in a percussion of joy. Tiny, downy feathers were floating in the air. Several older kids were in human form playing some arcane mixture of store, school, and doctor.

The spacious room itself was a charming mix of bold preschool decoration and the original saloon decor. The bar itself had been replaced with a row of low kitchen playware, but the original shelves remained behind it, crowded with stuffed animals and toys. Lit mirrors with arched tops above the shelves made the room look brighter and bigger than it was. There was a row of cages and cubbies backing the entryway wall, housing an array of classroom pets and a selection of birds who were chirping cheerfully into the chaos. A comparatively quiet nursery corner had several cribs surrounded by low walls and baby gates to keep disruptive older kids out. Heavy curtains could be drawn around the corner and there were rolled sleeping mats stuck in a wide bucket.

A reading corner by the nursery had shelves with board books along the bottom and paper books up higher. Big, fuzzy bean bags looked like inviting places to sit and cuddle with babies from the nursery or to read with older kids. There was one padded rocking chair as well. On the other side of the room were short tables and stacks of kid-sized chairs, plus a few highchairs. Locked storage cabinets were labeled with "Art supplies," "Glue and Paint," "Cleaning supplies," "Paper," and "Monsters! Stay out!"

A narrow hallway in the back led past two closed doors and opened out onto a high-fenced yard that let hints of sunlight and green-scented breeze spill in. One of the tables had been pulled and tipped over sideways to block the way to the hallway, and there was a stepladder filling the space. Addison had a glimpse of a very fine-looking ass in jeans that looked entirely too tight for carpentry. He was wearing only socks, out of respect to the no-shoes rules.

If Addison's instinct had been humming before, it was an electric sizzle now, and she wrestled her lynx's desire to caper without reason.

The rest of the man was up through the drop ceiling of the more modern rear of the building, cursing creatively. "Son of a monkey, I want to know what the guy who built this place was smoking."

"Son of a monkey!" one of the older children parroted. "Son of a monkey!"

"Smunky! Smunky!" a younger one echoed, and there was a chorus of nonsense from the school-grocery-hospital.

"Gaba!" the bobbing toddler at the door proclaimed generally. "Gaba!"

"You must be Addison!"

The woman who appeared from a back room past the ladder looked like a breath of fresh air in a checkered plaid shirt and a pair of age-softened jeans. Dark hair streaked with white and bright blue was pulled back in two ponytails that Addison's mother would have insisted were a sign that she was clinging too hard to youth.

Addison liked her at once.

"Yes, I'm here for the interview." She thrust a hand out and the woman, who could only be Cherry Aimes, shook it with a firm, kind handshake.

She didn't set off a shifter tingle of recognition, to Addison's surprise. Her cousin, a long-time resident of Nickel City, had told her about this job and recommended her for the position. Addison had assumed that someone running a day care specifically for shifters would be a shifter herself, but she didn't have that edge-of-the-senses prickle that all shifters shared.

Cherry looked at her hard and Addison felt like she was being evaluated in whole and hoped that she measured up. Her lynx was singing that this was where she belonged, this was the path to her happiness, that everything was right and true and *now*. It would be a shame if she blew that by falling on her face now.

"Would you mind skipping the interview and jumping right in with both feet?" Cherry asked plaintively. "My part-time help couldn't make it today, and we've had a plumbing emergency, and I got more kids today than I was expecting for our very first official day."

"N-not at all," Addison said. "Let's get started!" She was almost dizzy from the intensity of her instinct and the presence of so many young shifters.

Cherry gave her a slow, pleased grin, then called generally to the room, "Fingers and feet, everyone! Fingers and feet! I want you all to meet someone!" There was a big rectangular carpet in the middle marked on the edges with numbers and letters. "Everybody pick a letter!"

The bear cub turned into a boy of about four in coveralls and the dog he'd been wrestling was suddenly a slightly older girl wearing a sparkling skirt over a pair of jeans. The armadillo was abruptly a boy close to their age, stark naked. The owl flutter-skipped over to Cherry's feet and unfolded into a chubby toddler, reaching for her knees. The other children quickly gathered and claimed their letters, with a very brief struggle for the coveted "C," which had a picture of cherries.

The toddler guarding the gate seemed to realize that exciting things were happening without her and she gave a cry of protest, then let go of the gate to sink down to hands and knees and crawl to the colorful carpet, where one of the older children herded her to a letter and gave her a stuffed animal that temporarily mesmerized her.

"Thank you, everyone," Cherry said warmly. "Gil, what did you forget?"

Gil, the naked armadillo boy, looked down at himself in surprise. "CLOTHES!" he exclaimed. "I forgot my CLOTHES!"

"Please go find them," Cherry suggested. "We'll all wait, but I'm very excited to introduce you to our new teacher!"

Gil scampered into a corner where his forgotten clothing had clearly been accidentally shifted out of, while all the other children's attention settled on Addison, whose heart raced. They were a combination of curious and cautious. The owl-shifting toddler shuffled herself to the far side of Cherry, staring at Addison with round, golden-brown eyes.

Addison wiggled her fingers at the toddler, who giggled and hid her face against Cherry's leg.

Gil returned to the rug, awkwardly hopping on one leg as he tried to get his pants on the other leg. He took the letter "L."

"This is Teacher Addison," Cherry introduced. "I'd like you all to say hello."

It wasn't a terribly coherent hello chorus. Addison took mental note of which ones seemed exuberant and which acted shy. "You can call me Teacher Addy."

"I can add!" one of the boys volunteered enthusiastically. "Essept sevens."

"Sevens are very hard," Addison told him sympathetically. "I can help you remember them."

She was keenly aware of the scrutiny she was under, not only from the children, but from Cherry herself. She had gotten the interview easily, but she knew that it wasn't because of her qualifications; finding a shifter caretaker in a world where shifters were secret was tricky business. She might have been the only choice that Cherry had, and this was definitely a trial by fire. She was determined to prove that she was a good choice, not just a desperate one.

"I'd like you to teach her the rules, boys and girls," Cherry directed. "Some of you know them already. Tara, can you tell her the first rule of our school?"

Tara appeared to be one of the oldest girls, about five, with wavy brown hair and Asian features. She frowned self-consciously at the attention.

Before she could speak, Gil interrupted, "Fingers and FEET in FRONT OF PEOPLE!"

"I was going to say it," Tara protested, clearly hurt.

Gil didn't look particularly contrite.

"Let's go around and tell Teacher Addy your names," Cherry suggested. "Tara, would you like to start?"

Tara murmured her name at the floor in front of her.

"I'm GIL," the armadillo shifter shouted.

The boy next to him was Robert, and the dog shifter was Laura. Cherry introduced the owl-shifting toddler as Amy and Addison got a shy wave.

"That's Gabby," Cherry pointed.

The little girl who had greeted Addy when she arrived heard her name and abandoned the stuffy she had been examining to crawl in Addison's direction.

Addison sat down and Gabby went willingly into her lap, tugging experimentally at Addison's hair before snuggling happily into her arms. She wasn't a shifter, though she was close to the age that the transition usually happened.

"We've got two babies in the nursery right now," Cherry said, glancing towards the corner with the cribs. "Daria and Shane."

"Shane is my baby brother," Tara volunteered.

"Do you like being a big sister?" Addison asked her. "I was always the little sister."

Tara rewarded her with a slow smile.

In the hallway behind them, there was a sudden crash in the ceiling and swearing that had not been censored for children, followed by a swift, "Sorry, Cherry!"

"Let's go read a book!" Cherry suggested merrily. "How about a loud book?"

"TRAINS!" Gil hollered gamely.

Addison, still holding Gabby, helped corral the children over into the little library and sat to listen to a book with lots of audience participation and clapping. Gabby didn't pay a lot of attention to it, but she did like Addison's clapping and she joined in enthusiastically.

The little girl got restless during the next book, whining and straining in Addison's arms. Addison let her go, but Gabby immediately started to crawl for a gap by the table blocking the hallway towards the ladder. Addison laughed and chased her, swooping her up and making her chortle and shriek happily as the contractor started down the ladder, muttering and shaking his head.

Then he turned and looked at her, and Addison felt her giggles die at her lips.

It wasn't just he was genuinely breathtaking, with his warm, sepia skin and his jaw like a sculptor's dream. It wasn't even that he was a muscular specimen of male that transcended *guy* straight for *god.* It was that her instinct was humming in happiness and certainty, like she'd never felt it before.

3

*R*oderick knew he was staring, but it was impossible not to. Cherry's new hire was standing just across the table from him, holding his daughter in her strong arms and it was the most beautiful thing he'd ever seen. She had reddish-blonde hair in a sensible shoulder-length cut, pale, freckled skin, and a dimple in the middle of her chin. Her smile was crooked and eager, and she was wearing a blue skirt that looked green in the golden light from the back yard, over wild-patterned leggings.

She made his skin tingle, as every shifter did, but there was something more to his uncanny sudden awareness of her.

What is this...? He dived inward, calling for his inner wolf, as he folded the stepladder and moved aside the table.

Here, now, this, came the wolf's unhelpful answer. Roderick felt like his ears were pricked forward, his tail in a slow, eager wag, and he had to double-check to make sure his human body wasn't doing something ridiculous.

Every shifter had a sense of instinct. Just as certain birds knew when and how to migrate, and fish and turtles could find their way back to their birthplace, shifters had a subtle reaction to danger, a preternatural reflex that told them when something was wrong...and when something was right.

And oh, was this so *right.*

Some shifters—Roderick's mother included—believed in soulmates, in the possibility of finding that one true love, and recognizing them when they met.

"That doesn't mean there aren't other ways to find love," his mother had been swift to add, "or that you couldn't screw it up irredeemably with someone who might have been your perfect partner. It's just a little extra jumpstart to romance that comes along with being a shifter. You ever feel that instinct, you listen to it good, because magic whispers, it doesn't shout."

It was certainly whispering now, more loudly than he'd ever heard it, urging him to take a chance, to risk everything.

But he'd screwed up trying to follow his instinct before, and it was hard to think straight because she was so pretty and his senses were all jangling.

It wasn't just attraction, though certainly she was all that he'd ever fantasized, with curves everywhere they ought to be. But beyond lust, there was such a feeling of comfort, of coming home. She was safety and shelter and...

"Gaba!"

Gabby had grown impatient of them drinking each other in and was straining against the woman's grasp. "Abababa!"

"I think someone needs a new diaper," the woman said practically, a mixture of shyness and smiling that made Roderick's heart flip-flop.

So much for romance.

"I can do that," he offered, holding out his arms. Gabby stretched towards him, leaning without fear. "I haven't technically checked her in yet, so it's still on me."

"You don't have to do that," she protested, shifting her

grip on Gabby expertly so that she didn't fall. "It's my job…or at least, I hope it will be!"

"It's your first day," Roderick pointed out. "Cherry would never forgive me if I scared you away so soon."

"I *am* made of tougher stuff than that," she said, and her voice was made of laughter, but she offered him Gabby anyway.

She was, Roderick's instinct assured him. She was a coil of steel in silk, or a spicy candy, deceptively sweet and completely capable at the same time. He took Gabby, who babbled happily at the exchange. "Gababa babby."

"I'm Roderick," he said, tucking Gabby into one elbow and extending his other hand.

"Addison." She took his hand in a long, slow handshake that made his soul sing, and they smiled at each other foolishly. "The kids call me Teacher Addy."

"Addy," Gabby said firmly.

Roderick gave her a skeptical look. Gabby had been babbling for several months now, but it was hard to pick firm words out of the nonsense. Probably these were just random syllables, like adda *probably* wasn't dada, yet.

Addison laughed again, softly, and shook her head as she took her hand back self-consciously. "It's most likely…"

"…Just random babble," Roderick finished for her. "She's not really doing words or names yet, even though she has a lot to say. She's a gabby Gabby."

Now who was babbling?

Gabby was getting impatient and uncomfortable. "Ababa dabby!"

"Duty calls," Roderick said, only hearing how it sounded after it was out of his mouth.

"Duty does," Addison giggled, with a long ooo on the u.

Diaper jokes, Roderick thought. He'd just met the woman

who completed him, and he was grinning with her over *diaper jokes.*

"Gababa," Gabby complained.

He forced himself not to look back over his shoulder to see if Addison was watching him as he carried Gabby to the little bathroom in the back of the day care. It wasn't the worst diaper she'd ever supplied for him, and he cleaned her up efficiently.

"Well, Gabby," he said as he wiped her down. "What do you make of this new development in our lives?"

Now that he wasn't directly facing Addison, doubts were crowding back as instinct ebbed in intensity. He'd been led down the wrong path before.

"Adaba bah," Gabby said conversationally.

"It does kind of complicate things," Roderick pointed out. "I mean, I hadn't really thought about dating again. Do you like her? Because it looks like you might see a lot more of her than I am." Was he actually jealous of a fourteen-month-old?

"Tuh-tuh," Gabby said, pointing at a turtle on the wall above the changing table. "Moo."

"Instinct isn't always *right,*" he told her, snapping the legs of her romper closed again. "Or at least, I haven't always been right about it. But I've got such a *good* feeling about this." A good feeling didn't tell him *how* to go about things; he knew it was possible to drive her away as easily as it was to win her heart. Instinct couldn't make up for sheer stupidity. Dana was proof of that.

Roderick wondered what Addison would make of him talking to Gabby like she was a grown-up, holding her own end of the conversation. All the baby books said it was good for their language skills and he didn't like to leave the television on, so he'd cultivated the habit when she was an infant, but he yearned for the day that she responded with more than strung-together syllables.

"Ababa boo," Gabby said reassuringly, and she gurgled happily as Roderick swung her up into her arms again.

"Let's go see Teacher Addy," Roderick said, wondering if she would echo the name again.

"Gabba," Gabby agreed. "Tuh-tuh."

Roderick's instinct suddenly gave a twang of unexpected warning and he rushed from the bathroom to find Addison at the front of the day care by the room divider, saying in alarm, "You can't come back here! No shoes are allowed back here, please! Let me get Cherry for you!" There was a note of panic and desperation to her voice, as well as understandable uncertainty.

A familiar voice said shrilly, "I don't know who you are, but I have every right to come in, and my boots won't hurt anything, don't be so *fussy*. Oh, just move!"

Veronica Chase, with her too-tight jeans and too-styled hair, looked appallingly overdone next to Addison's playful, easy beauty. She was stepping over the baby gate with her gold-etched cowboy boots, all but pushing Addison out of the way and Roderick glanced over the playroom to see in alarm that several of the children were in animal form. Cherry was busy in the nursery with a wailing baby.

In an instant, he was striding to intercept the woman at the gate, crowding up close as if he had no concept of personal space. He didn't mind being that close to Addison, but Veronica's proximity made his skin prickle in completely different ways. This woman was trouble, from her salon-styled bob to her ridiculous boots.

He didn't need instinct to tell him that, though. "Oh, Veronica," he said with a growl. "I had a chance to look at that leak. Let's have a word about the work that will need to be done. Out *here*."

4

It wasn't that Addison needed or wanted a big, strong, handsome guy to come to rescue her, but she had to admit that it kind of took her breath away when Gabby's gorgeous dad came and growled down the woman trying to push her way in. He *literally* growled at her, and Addison took entirely too much pleasure from the woman's look of affront.

Gabby made raspberries at her that were probably completely coincidental and growled in imitation. She seemed considerably happier now, and Addison found it hard to blame her. She'd be pretty happy in Roderick's arms, too.

She jerked her thoughts back to the confrontation in front of her.

"I found the problem, Veronica," Roderick was saying as he stepped in front of Addison. He put a weird emphasis on the name, and it was the second time he'd said it. "You've got a whole section of plumbing that isn't up to code, and there are probably more leaks just waiting to happen. What you really want to do is get in there and replace all the fittings, before you have an even bigger problem." He was angling the woman away, and Addison caught the barest edge of a shoulder shrug to her.

She understood his hint at once. Veronica wasn't a shifter, and her instinct to keep her out had been solid. She slid away, letting Roderick keep their unwelcome visitor at the room divider, and went back into the nursery to warn Cherry.

"There's a woman named Veronica who is trying to come back," she said, glancing around. "She had a key, I didn't buzz her in!"

Cherry grimaced. "Veronica Chase," she said with a sigh. "She owns all the buildings on this block and the main street one block over. She thinks that means free rein in any of them, at any time."

"Does she know…?"

Cherry shook her head and they quickly took stock of the children. Most of them were playing in human form, but Amy was hopping around as an owl and Gil was naked again.

Without consulting, they divided the tasks. "Fingers and feet, kids!" Cherry called cheerfully, as if it was nothing more than a nursery rhyme. "Fingers and feet!" She knelt to coax Amy back into human form as Addison went to find where Gil had shed his clothing and get him dressed again.

She left him tugging his shirt on to hurry back with Amy's clothing and found that it was too late.

Amy was still an owl, and Veronica Chase was coming into the room, with Roderick at her heels looking like a thundercloud. Addison noticed that she was still wearing her boots.

Cherry looked up and waved. "We're having a zoo day!" she called cheerfully. Unable to persuade Amy to shift, she had opened the cage doors for some of the real animals and gathered them on the carpet with the toddler shifter. A rabbit and a guinea pig were sniffing around, while Tara squealed and tried to pet them, and a large, slow lizard was testing the air with its tongue.

Veronica's gaze swept right over Amy without even noticing her. "You realize that you'll lose your deposit if I have to replace the flooring," she said with distaste.

"Of course," Cherry agreed mildly. "This is one of those protective waterproof carpets; the floor underneath should be fine, even if there's an accident."

The lizard started to creep slowly for the perimeter, and Veronica backed up with a hiss of disgust.

"The REAL ANIMALS!" Gil shouted, pushing around Addison to plop down in the middle of the carpet and try to pet the guinea pig. At least he was wearing his clothing again.

"I'm petting that one," Tara protested.

Robert, drawn from the library by Gil's loud pronouncement, came yelling into the circle as Addison tried to calm him. "We have to be gentle, Robert!" she reminded him. "Don't frighten the animals!" *Or Amy,* she added in her mind. The last thing they wanted was for the little girl to shift into human form right in front of Veronica.

"Did you need something?" Cherry asked Veronica pointedly. "We're in the middle of zoo day."

"Someone's liable to be bit," Veronica sniffed.

Personally, Addison hoped it was her.

"My contractor tells me that you need some plumbing fixes made," the odious woman went on. "But he says they are optional, and if I pay him to do them, I'll have to increase your rent."

Roderick sputtered. "That's not what I said."

"Optional," Veronica repeated. Then her voice sweetened. "But if it doesn't cost too much, of course, I wouldn't have to do that. I could take a small loss this month if I had to."

Addison was appalled. Even she could see that Veronica

was playing them against each other, forcing Roderick to a lower price or Cherry to higher rent. Everyone knew it and could do nothing about it.

Gabby spotted Amy at that moment. "Abababababa!" she said, stretching her arms for the tiny owl chick.

Amy hopped up and down in recognition and Roderick, assessing the situation, swiftly said, "Let's talk about the invoice out here, Veronica."

Veronica, sensing a win, turned away just as Amy shifted into a naked toddler, lost her balance, fell over backward, and burst out crying in surprise.

Addison dashed in, swept Amy into her arms, and got a shirt over her head in one swift motion as Veronica glanced back with a look of annoyance.

Veronica looked a little puzzled, but when her gaze swept down over the animals, she noticed that the lizard had advanced further on her and she gave a dramatic shudder and retreated out into the entry, muttering about chickens. Cherry took Gabby from Roderick and he followed her out.

Gabby, abandoned by her father, gave a wail of outrage, and Cherry and Addison breathed a sigh of relief.

"What a landlord," Addison said in an undertone, as she got a diaper on Amy and finished dressing her.

"She's a real piece of work," Cherry agreed. "But it was hard to find a place with a truly private back yard like this place has, that was central to where parents were working. Veronica owns a lot of property in town, and this was the only place I could afford." She smiled. "Besides, look at this great place."

Addison smiled up at the rough-cut ceilings, thick wood beams full of character, and the old bar features. "It's really perfect," she agreed. It had the kind of wear and weather that wouldn't bother children, and it was just the right size and configuration.

Roderick came back and Addison felt like he had brought sunshine back with him. He took Gabby easily from Cherry and tossed her a few inches in the air to turn her tears to squeals of joy.

"You shouldn't charge that woman less because of me," Cherry protested.

Roderick scowled. "That woman shouldn't pass that kind of cost on to you in the first place," he said. "It *should* have been done right to begin with." His face softened. "I'm still getting paid enough," he promised. "Not every job has to be at union rates."

Amy squirmed in Addison's arms and she put the toddler back on the floor so she could stagger to the bunny and sink down in a squat beside her to pat her ears with exaggerated gentleness.

Cherry rounded up the lizard and the guinea pig and put them back into their cages. The kids were reluctant to say goodbye to the rabbit. Cherry appeased them by letting them push lettuce in through the bars for her to eat.

Addison barely noticed, absolutely entranced by Roderick with Gabby in his arms. Like a sleepwalker, she closed the distance between them. She said quietly, "Thank you for the distraction. That was a close thing, with Amy."

"You acted quickly," he said, admiringly. "And Veronica can be a lot to handle."

"Instinct told me she was trouble the moment I saw her," Addison confessed, wondering if she put too much emphasis on the first word. "But I doubted it. I mean, I don't know anyone here and she had a *key*. Maybe she was someone Cherry knew..."

"Instinct was right in this case."

The air between them seemed to charge. Addison's skin was humming now, too strong to ignore, and she knew she was gazing at him besottedly.

They might have had that conversation then, the *you-and-me?* talk, the acknowledgment that they both felt something amazing, because it was really hard to deny that they were both feeling something amazing...but there was a sudden commotion in the school behind her, and the phone in Roderick's pocket gave a demanding buzz.

"I should get back to work," she said regretfully.

"I have another job I need to get to," he said, sounding every drop as regretful.

He started to leave, then turned back as he realized he was still holding Gabby. "You have to stay here, sweetie."

The hand-off was complicated by the fact that Gabby realized she was going to be left behind again and took double handfuls of everything she could reach. Roderick had to pry her off and transfer her, wailing and sobbing, to Addison, who had to take her without succumbing to her own desire to climb into Roderick's arms.

"I feel your pain," she murmured to Gabby, who wanted no part of her and actively tried to push off with all of her considerable strength.

Roderick stepped over the gate and stuffed his feet into his boots as Addison turned away, neither of them wishing to draw out their goodbye and prolong Gabby's misery.

Gabby settled almost as soon as he was out of sight, but fussed when Addison offered to put her down on the floor, so Addison carried her around with her for most of the morning.

5

For Roderick, walking away and leaving Gabby with someone else was always like being stretched on a medieval torture device.

Walking away and leaving Gabby with someone else when she was upset and crying piteously for him was like being doused in hot sauce after he'd been flayed. Even knowing that her protests rarely lasted long after he was out of sight was small comfort for the distress he was causing her.

Leaving her with Addison felt complicated because he didn't want to leave either of them, but he also knew, completely, that Gabby would be safe with her, safer than anywhere else in the whole world that wasn't his own arms.

Instinct could find him his soulmate, his mother had said. She hated the term mate and thought it made it sound like it was all about sex. "It's not about sex," she'd said frankly. Then, to his mortification, she had laughed. "Well, it's not all about the sex. It's about compatibility."

Addison...it was like she was a fit to all the puzzle pieces in his life. She could be the companion his life lacked, the breath of fresh air his stale existence desperately needed. She could be the mother that Gabby didn't have.

Roderick got into his pickup and paused without turning it on, still hearing the echo of Gabby's cries echoing in his ears.

Hadn't instinct told him that Dana was right, too? He'd thought that she was his one forever, and had trusted that they could get past their differences, if they both worked at it, and that they would make a life together. But the life that Dana had wanted wasn't what he had envisioned, and she didn't think there was a place for him, let alone for a child, which was something that Roderick didn't think he could ever forgive her for. Instinct had gone cold, like he'd been wrong about it all along.

So what if he was wrong about this, too? The sense was never obvious. It was a quiet whisper, a promise...but promises could be broken and Roderick didn't necessarily trust himself after the disaster of his last relationship. He'd never been sure if the magic had been flawed, if he'd misinterpreted it, or if he'd done something wrong. If he'd fought harder to stay together, if he'd been more accommodating...

The phone beside him rang, jolting him from his spiral of introspection and doubt.

"Douglass Plumbing," he answered.

It was an unfamiliar number and an unfamiliar voice, but a very familiar request.

"I've got a quick install job to do in that neighborhood," Roderick said, consulting his schedule. He liked an old-fashioned written calendar, and had a black-covered day planner that he laughingly called his little black book; plumbing jobs were as close to a relationship as he'd gotten to romance since Dana left. "I can be there about three o'clock."

He penciled them in and hung up, then finally started the pickup and pulled out into the quiet street.

"Hot Rod!" he was greeted at the door of his first job. "How's it hanging?"

Roderick had heard all the 'rod' jokes, but Ian Gadsby never tired of them. "I'm here to tighten your drains," he said mockingly, and they exchanged a rough, friendly hug before Ian stepped aside to let him in.

"Just be careful not to flush Lucy down the toilet, or let her climb into your toolbox. I spent two hours yesterday trying to find her while she was sleeping on top of the fridge."

"She's shifting now?"

"Yup. A squirrel like her mother was and as fast as a streak. I thought it got challenging when she learned how to walk, but let me tell you, this wall-climbing thing is giving me white hairs. How's Gabby?"

"Still only two legs," Roderick said with relief. "How's the writing going?"

Ian grimaced. "Not well. Lucy isn't napping so much now and I feel like I'm chasing her every moment I'm awake."

"Have you thought about putting her in day care? Cherry's got her business license and her shifter-watching is all official and aboveboard now. Well, the shifters part is hush-hush, of course, but the business is legal."

"It's tempting," Ian said wistfully. "I don't know if I'd be able to afford it, did I tell you that my landlord is planning to sell the house? Apparently, Veronica Chase is buying up a bunch of property in the area and made him a deal he can't refuse."

Roderick frowned, remembering Veronica's smug expression when she talked him into taking less for the repair job than he knew he should charge.

Ian shook his head. "Besides, I feel like since I work from home, I ought to be able to keep her here with me. Even if it's really hard getting anything done with interruptions every ten minutes to pull her off the top of the bookshelf or pry her out of the box she's gotten stuck in. And I worry, man, she can get into anything if I look away for a minute. Or out of anything." He gazed around the room. "Lucy!" he called, looking around at the tops of bookcases. "Honey? Remember Mr. Roderick?"

With just a squeak of warning, there was suddenly a tiny furry body launching itself at Roderick and he dropped his toolbox to catch a toddler, a little older than Gabby, as she shifted from a little reddish squirrel to a girl...right on his shoulder.

"Hot Rod!" she said in excitement, wrapping her arms around his head. "Gabby's daddy! Play with Gabby!"

"You forgot your clothes, Lucy," Ian said, mortified. "Let's go put them on again."

"You know, they teach clothing shifting at Cherry's," Roderick said, laughing as he handed off the little girl and picked up his toolbox again. "I can find the bathroom while you do that."

Clogged toilets were the least glamorous part of his work and honestly the most reliable pay because kids would put anything they could fit down them...and plenty that didn't. Roderick gave it a test flush, watching its slow progress, listening to the drain in the sink for clues to the location of the clog, and went to his truck to get the snake.

It was a simple job, and the clog pushed through without trouble. Roderick didn't even have to open up a pipe cleanout to get it cleared and he was done in a matter of minutes. "No charge," he said, shaking his head when Ian reached for his wallet. Lucy was dressed in a purple dress covered in little rainbow-maned unicorns and was sitting deceptively quietly on the couch, her bare toes wiggling as she flipped through a picture book. "Just keep me in mind when you have a real problem that I can charge you the moon for."

"I wouldn't take my business anywhere else," Ian promised, keeping his gaze knowingly on Lucy as they moved towards the door. When they were out of easy earshot, he asked, "So, is it still just Cherry with her daycare? I mean, I feel like I ought to be able to manage writing with just one small kid around, but maybe it would be nice if Lucy had more playtime. I do have a deadline coming up."

"She's got Shea Ando part time, and...it looks like she just hired someone new full time," Roderick said. Remembering how Addison had looked holding Gabby made him smile foolishly.

He hesitated, then asked, "Do you believe in...soulmates?"

"Like that mate nonsense that shifter girls sigh over?" Ian mocked. "True love and destiny," he said in a falsetto.

Roderick wasn't sure exactly what his face did then, but Ian didn't miss it. He sobered quickly. "The new hire at Cherry's day care? You think she's the one?"

"I guess there's no way to be sure," Roderick said sheepishly. It was sort of ridiculous to feel this crazy for someone he'd just met. Was it really a whisper of magic, or just a pretty face at a vulnerable moment? He felt full of bubbles, half-drunk with anticipation, and his wolf was wagging his tail in glee.

"So, tell me about her!" Roderick had all of Ian's attention now. "A shifter, I'm guessing?"

"Yes, but I don't know what. We've barely had a chance to talk. It was like recognizing another shifter, you know, but dialed up to eleven. I looked at her and...had feelings. I don't even know."

"She's hot?"

Roderick bristled. "That's not what this was. It was...more

like hearing a song on the radio that you've been trying to remember for a year, or suddenly getting a joke."

"So, not hot?"

Roderick realized that Ian was teasing him, grinning knowingly. "She's hot," he said, shaking his head. "Kind of like a sexy Miss Frizzle mixed with Mary Poppins. Definitely a spoonful of sugar."

"Is it sadder that I know those references, or that they appeal to me?"

Roderick chuckled. "Nah, it's a single dad thing."

But he didn't want to be a single dad, Roderick realized rather suddenly. He wanted to go home to someone. And he wanted Gabby to have more than just him to look up to. Could he trust that Addison was that person? Was instinct enough for something *that* important? It hadn't been able to steer him right with Dana, after all.

"Lucy? Lucy?" Ian suddenly swiveled and looked back at the couch...where Lucy's book had been set aside and her unicorn dress lay empty. "Son of a..."

"Monkey," Roderick provided. "Son of a monkey."

"I gotta go find my monkey," Ian said. "Before she gets into the cleaning supplies or eats the taxes or something. Thanks for the plunge."

"Any time."

When Roderick shut the door behind him, he heard Ian calling, "Lucy? Who's the best squirrel? Who gets nuts for dinner if she comes out right *now?*"

6

Addison spent the lunch period ripping the tops off yogurt tubes and opening lids. The range of dexterity was challenging, from kids who could manage their entire meal without assistance to toddlers in high chairs who were still exploring textures and smashing berries on their trays. As the older kids finished, Cherry had them clean their placemats, put away their lunch bags, and wash their hands.

"Who's ready to practice shifting?" she asked enthusiastically.

"I AM!" Gil called from his cubby, standing on tip-toe to shove his bag into the space above his coat hook with no care for the art papers that were already there.

"What are you going to remember this time?" Cherry teased him.

"My CLOTHES!" Gil laughed.

"Will you be alright here with these guys?" Cherry asked Addison, who was trying to convince one of the littlest children that berries were not better served on the floor. "I know I'm asking a lot for what was supposed to be a casual interview. This was not the day I had planned."

Addison wanted badly to impress Cherry, but she paused to evaluate before she agreed too eagerly. The two babies were sleeping soundly, absolutely oblivious to the surrounding chaos, and there were only two toddlers remaining: Gabby and the shy owl shifter. One older girl, Tara, was dawdling over her food.

"No problem," Addison said confidently.

Cherry traipsed outside with the rest of the children and the comparative quiet in their wake was remarkable, even though their shouts and laughter could still be heard down the back hallway. Addison got several more mouthfuls of berries into actual mouths and chased them with cubes of cheese that were met with disdain until she pretended to eat them herself.

"So delicious," she said, closing her eyes and rubbing her stomach. The word delicious on her tongue made her think about the contractor, Roderick. What would he be doing now? When would they next have a chance to talk? "I love cheese so much! I'm going to steal it all!"

This had the toddlers hurrying to clear their trays, giggling and grabbing at their food with clumsy fingers as they stuffed it in their mouths.

Addison took the top level of their trays and brought warm, damp washcloths that were as much for amusement as they were for cleaning, swiping at faces and fingers in laughing games of peekaboo.

She finally released them from their high chairs and let them continue their chaos with the soft blocks while she washed the trays with half an eye back on their play.

Tara was still lingering over her lunch, eating one careful raisin at a time from the little cardboard box.

"Don't you want to go outside and shift with the other kids?" Addison asked as she wiped the table around her lunch mat.

Tara seemed to hunch up a little smaller, looking miserable in the way that kids that age couldn't hide. "I'm still eating," she protested.

"You could save the rest for your afternoon snack," Addison suggested. "You don't want to miss all the fun."

She remembered the shifter games she'd played as a child, games designed to practice speed shifting, and the ability to do it in motion. There were tag games—shift-is-safe—and variations of Simon Says. Some of them were fast and dizzy, did Tara like quieter games? Maybe Tara wasn't very good at shifting yet, too slow for games, or frequently forgetting her clothing.

Was she being bullied by the other children? She doubted that Cherry would allow that to happen in her care.

"We could practice shifting in here, if you wanted," Addison offered warmly, sitting in the uncomfortably small chair across from her. "Gabby, please don't touch Amy if she doesn't like it!"

Tara only ate slower, and after a moment, sullenly shook her head, whispering something that Addison couldn't hear over the sudden cries of the toddlers. She stood up to moderate their argument over a coveted toy, and when she returned, Tara was still picking at her food.

She sat beside Tara this time. "What's up, buttercup? Do you like to shift?"

Tara's expressive face brightened at the cute name but fell again at once. "I'm ugly," she said despondently.

Addison felt her heart twinge in sympathy.

"Oh, honey—" she started.

Then Gil came running in, stark naked, shouting, "I have to use the POTTY!"

Addison swiftly stood to close the door to the little bathroom behind him and while she was doing that, Tara packed up her lunch and the rest of the class came streaming in, laughing and full of energy. One of the boys was carrying Gil's forgotten clothes.

Just then, a baby woke, squalling in dismay. Addison went to scoop her up and check her diaper as Cherry began the herculean task of getting a half-dozen wound-up children to calm down for story time. Tara sat quietly with the others, waiting for the book to begin.

7

Cherry took her aside early that afternoon when the children were down for their quiet time. "You've been great, can you stay the rest of the day and then we can talk about the paperwork and pay and hours and all that? I'm happy to include today in your pay for this period, of course."

Addy felt a thrill of triumph, followed by a moment of uncertainty. She already loved Cherry's day care and every one of the kids, from precocious Amy to the very loud Gil who couldn't remember his clothes. She liked Cherry's policies, and the way she handled the children; she knew this would be a good place to work, a place where she could make a difference in people's lives, where she could teach and nurture. And most of all, she liked Cherry herself, with her unflappable humor and easy smile.

But Addison didn't have a place to live yet and agreeing to this job meant *committing*. This wasn't an under-the-table barista job that she could pick up and leave without notice. That was something she'd had to do before, but she didn't want to do that to Cherry.

The job also meant staying in Nickel City, and seeing Gabby's gorgeous dad again nearly every single day.

She realized that she hadn't answered Cherry yet, conflicted and swimming in feelings, with instinct like the hum of distracting electric lights confusing matters even further. Instinct didn't understand things like W2s or bills or stalker ex-boyfriends who hired private investigators. "I'll stay the day," she said cautiously. She wasn't promising anything long-term, not yet. She could spend the rest of the afternoon deciding for sure.

The children, however, had other plans for her, and instead of carefully pondering her options, Addy spent the remainder of the day running from diaper emergency to squalling baby, feeding, cleaning, and playing endless games of make-believe mixed up with math and letters and logic.

Once almost all the kids had been picked up, there was a lull in the activity and Addy immediately started searching real estate listings on her phone.

Nickel City had a fair amount of sprawling suburbs full of trees, it seemed, but there weren't a lot of apartments. Addy looked at some of the ads for cute little places with fenced yards and wondered what it would be like to have a place like that. She could even get a pet! She had always wanted a dog.

Then she looked at the prices of the rentals and regretfully browsed away. The apartment options were small and disappointingly overpriced. Addy had done a little research months ago, before coming all this way from New York state, but she must have misremembered the prices; it seemed like they were noticeably higher than she recalled.

"How was your first day?" Cherry asked from the doorway, one eye over her shoulder for trouble; the remaining children seemed to be playing peacefully. "You didn't run away screaming."

"Well, no one had to go to the hospital, except for the

pretend one, so it wasn't too bad," Addy said, putting her phone politely away. "I don't suppose you know anyone looking to let a room? Wendy is going to want me off her couch soon. I thought it would be a lot cheaper to rent in a small town than it was in the city, but I'm finding that's not really the case." She wanted the job and the excuse to stay in Nickel City and see Roderick again, but it wouldn't really cover the cost of a place unless she could find a roommate or two. Maybe she could pick up some part-time work in the evenings?

Cherry glowered fiercely. "A lot of people I know have mentioned that their landlords have been raising the rent lately. I guess they've been getting sweet offers to sell."

"That Veronica woman who was here earlier?"

"She's the worst," Cherry confirmed. "She's setting up a bunch of short-term rentals that are crowding neighbors out of their communities to make a tidy profit. Nickel City got a little press a year or so ago when it won some kind of prettiest town in Montana nonsense, and it made some big lists for places to go antiquing. The extra tourism has been nice for the economy, but it's not so great for keeping secrets, and it has other downsides, apparently. Grace, at the Mine Hotel, actually says that she's doing worse business than ever, because everyone is renting full houses for not that much more than she charges for a room, and they don't have to meet the same kind of hospitality restrictions she does."

"Aren't there regulations that prohibit short-term rentals in neighborhoods?"

"Nickel City has never needed them before now," Cherry said, shaking her head. "We were off the radar of everything until we were suddenly in the running for town popularity contests or whatever. Oh, whoops, hang on." She went to untangle Gabby from the cord of the play telephone she was trying to use upside-down; it was too short to choke her, but she was getting frustrated trying to work the device. Tara was playing quietly with a doctor's kit and a stuffed animal and the remaining baby was wiggling on blankets and reaching for enrichment toys inside the safe-for-babies play area.

"Let me show you the shutdown routine and explain how the door lock works. You'll need to download an app to your phone in order to check the camera! And then I've got paperwork for you sign and we can talk about the work hours!"

Cherry walked Addison through sterilizing the toys and bathroom, vacuuming, and showed her the check-in system, each parent and authorized guardian carefully noted by each child. There were only nine on the roster so far. Roderick Douglass was the name by Gabby's. No one else. Addison didn't think that he would have looked at her quite like that if he was *married,* but it had occurred to her more than once throughout the day that it was possible Gabby's mother was still in the picture somehow and she could not help but wonder how she would fit into that puzzle.

Cherry gave her the paperwork in her little private office and left her alone in the room while she watched the rest of the kids.

Addison read through the contract, which laid out the hours (plenty!) and benefits (nothing fancy) and the pay (a fair wage) and paused to listen for clues from her instinct.

And then she smiled, because she didn't need instinct to tell her that this was where she wanted to be. "Keep your secrets," she told her lynx, and she signed the papers with an extra flourish and went out to help pack up the next child who was going home.

Every time that the door chime rang, Addison's heart started pounding, and she eagerly looked, hoping to see Gabby's handsome hunk of a dad again. She signed out the other children, memorizing faces and names so that she could safely hand them over or buzz them in without checking with Cherry or seeing their ID in the future, and gave out warm hugs to the kids as they left. They seem to have gleefully accepted her as Teacher Addy and she was excited by the prospect of working here indefinitely...as long as she could afford it. As long as *Cherry* could afford it, with only nine kids enrolled, especially since the schedule indicated that not all of them were full-time.

"Here's a question for you," Cherry said, coming out of the bathroom to stash the cleaning supplies in a locked cabinet out of reach. There was a bottle of very diluted bleach left in reach of the older kids for wiping down placemats and art tables, but everything else was secured.

Addison tickled the baby with a gentle, socked toe. "Sure."

"Do you like A Flower Garden Day Care, or Little Haven for the name of the business?"

"I thought it was just going to be called Cherry's," Addison said in surprise. "That's what everyone has called it."

"I worry that it sounds like a strip club," Cherry said frankly. "And we're already set up in a saloon!"

Addison could not help laughing. The baby at her feet looked up in surprise and broke into a big toothless grin, then farted loudly.

Cherry and Addison both chuckled at that. "Well, I know his opinion," Cherry quipped.

Addison didn't hear the door chime over their laughter, but her lynx suddenly sat up within her and began to purr. She checked the phone app with her heart in her throat, and nearly fell down on top of the baby when her whole world seemed to tilt at the sight of Gabby's dad at the door, straightening his collar like he was arriving for a date.

She tried to stuff her giddiness down. "Gabby, your daddy's here!"

Addison herded Gabby towards the entranceway, walking her with each of her hands in her own.

He was waiting in the doorway to the lobby, obviously not wanting to take off the heavy boots that were forbidden in the back area, and he crouched to meet her. "Hey, pup!"

Gabby had no shame in her delight at the sight of him and she screamed in joy and excitement, pulling her hands free of Addison's to sway in place and then throw herself down to crawl to him. He pulled her up over the gate into his embrace effortlessly.

Addison was busy trying not to scream in delight and crawl to him herself, then remembered that she had an excuse to talk to him. Cherry handed her the checkout clipboard with a tolerant, knowing smile. Cherry might not be a shifter, but Addison was sure that her flushed face and stupid smile were obvious clues for humans, too.

"I'll need you to sign her out," she stammered when she had closed the distance to the gate.

And Roderick looked up from Gabby and *smiled* at her.

Not just a smile, but a whole face glow like she'd just said something clever, which she clearly had not. He was as ridiculously handsome as he'd been that morning, and Addison thought that her knees felt as weak as Gabby's.

"Do you need to see ID?" he asked, in that gruff, teasing voice.

"No! No, I saw you this morning, I mean, and Cherry okayed you, and Gabby obviously...ah..." Was coherency too much to ask of herself? Addison wondered.

Gabby was laughing and babbling. She looked at Addison and said, "Gabba abby ADDY!" as she pulled on Roderick's collar. It was probably still just nonsense, not actually her name.

"Uh, her diaper bag is hanging there," Addison pointed out. "And let me just see if there were any notes..." If anything came up during the day—how long they napped, if a kid didn't like their lunch, or if something got damaged, or if there were any concerns at all—Cherry's form had a place to write a quick note to pass on to the approved grown-up.

"'Ask for his number,'" Addison read before she bothered to make sense of Cherry's swiftly written words. "Oh."

She looked up in mortification to find that Roderick's smile had split into a broad grin.

"I mean, I uh, have it here for your emergency contact," Addison floundered. "But that's obviously not, I mean, for personal use." She was such an idiot.

Gabby had enjoyed her fill of hugs and she struggled for freedom, arching herself backward and pushing away. "Abba gabba babba OOOOO!" Roderick tickled her to giggles and flipped her upside down to turn them into shrieks of delight.

"I'd like it if you did," Roderick said to Addison.

"Did what?" What was *he* thinking about? She knew what she was thinking about, and it made her entire body flush.

"Use my number for personal use."

"You want me to call you?"

"Or I could call you," Roderick suggested. "But I don't have your number."

"I could give it to you," Addison said swiftly.

"I'd like it if you did," Roderick said a second time, and they both laughed.

The most remarkable part of the whole ridiculous conversation was that he looked every bit as pole-axed as Addy felt, sort of stunned and gorgeous all at once, with a big wide smile like he'd just been given the best present in the world.

Addison had once been at a shifter friend's home in northern Wisconsin during a big snowstorm, and she'd stolen a chance to shift into lynx form and dive out into a yard full of deep, fluffy snow. It was better than swimming, rolling around in her cat form, leaping and batting at clumps of snow. She felt like that now, fun and free and entirely new. The play had all been...*instinctive.*

Her shifter instinct told her to trust, to make this leap. Roderick would catch her, just like he caught Gabby, and they could have the whole world.

8

*I*f it weren't for Gabby, squirming and laughing in his arms, Roderick might have kissed Addison right then and there, just on the strength of her gaze. She was looking up at him, with those sparkling eyes, like she was standing on a cliff of anticipation, poised to jump.

What was her shift form? he wondered, but it was considered impolite to ask among shifters.

Unfortunately, he needed at least one free hand to put her number in his phone, and when he reached for it, Gabby gave a herculean surge in her effort to escape. It took both limbs and tucking her backward under his elbow, tickling her to distract her, before he could extract his phone from a pocket.

He unlocked it and tossed it to Addison, who caught it in surprise. Did she think he was a complete knucklehead because he was having difficulties holding onto a twenty-pound squirming child? Gabby seemed to be doing her best to embarrass him, struggling mightily.

He righted Gabby and got her bag, bouncing her in his arms. "We're going to go home and have blueberries," he promised, which made her eyes get big. She smiled and was more cooperative after that, making the sign for *more.*

Addison had tapped her number into his contacts, and she shyly handed the phone back. "I didn't realize that she knew signs," she said, and she put her hand to the side of her head and then waved with it before giving a thumbs up with her free hand and pointing to Gabby. *Hello, how are you?*

"A little," Roderick said. "I learned some from YouTube. I heard that kids could get frustrated with speech before they were really verbal, and it seemed useful to know a few things. We use *more* a lot, *milk, yes, no*...lots of *nos.*"

"A lot of early educators use it now," Addison said approvingly, and Roderick felt like he'd been patted on the head. His wolf's tail was a metronome in his head.

Gabby looked back and forth between them, her brow furrowed. "Gababa," she interjected in protest. She wanted her promised blueberries.

Roderick slipped the phone back into his pocket and wished he had something half as intelligent to say to Addison. "So, I'll call you," he said, sounding like a complete dork.

"I'd like it if you did," Addison said with a giggle, and even though it was clearly the dumbest joke in the world at this point, Roderick gave a laugh that was too loud in the quiet entry and embarrassed himself.

"So," he said awkwardly, "Yeah, I guess I'll talk to you later."

She waved with her fingers, clutching the clipboard at her chest, with a big smile and bright eyes. Roderick forced himself to turn away and go.

Gabby wanted nothing to do with the car seat, struggling and whining as he buckled her into it. He distracted her with one of the many toys strewn across the bench seat. He'd bought a crew cab years ago thinking it might be useful for a plumbing crew. He just hadn't expected the crew to turn out to be one opinionated little girl who ruled with a drooly fist and could be football-carried under one arm.

"Let's go home and get you some blueberries," he said, once he had triumphed over her capture in the hated harness.

"Abbabbagab," she said in frustration, and she threw the stuffed turtle, then screamed because she couldn't reach it.

Roderick reached down, picked the turtle off the seat, and returned it to her. "I can't do that while I'm driving," he reminded her. He piled the rest of her toys in with her, even knowing that it wouldn't matter if she had a dozen other toys if she lost the one she wanted.

She was asleep almost before he had pulled away from the front of Cherry's still-unnamed day care.

Gabby slept the entire drive and stirred only minimally when Roderick unbuckled her and lifted her out of the car seat. She was starting to get big for the back-facing seat, but he had read that they were safer until they were two.

She woke up clingy and wanted to snuggle with Roderick, so he kept her in one arm while he puttered around the kitchen, heating the oven for his dinner and setting her food out on her highchair tray. It was slower working one-handed than putting her down, but he knew from experience that she would cry if he did that, and a later dinner seemed like a smaller price to pay.

"Is crabby Gabby ready for some blueberries?" he wanted to know, putting his phone on the counter longingly. Addison's number was in there, and he was dying to call her and hear her laugh again.

Gabby fussed a little when he clipped her into the highchair but was quickly distracted by the blueberries. She agreed to eat some of the cold elbow noodles he scooped out of the container in the fridge and chased a few garbanzo beans around without interest.

A week ago, she'd wanted nothing but garbanzo beans. Roderick had two cases of them now and feared they'd never get through them. When he pulled his own dinner out of the oven, she signed *mine* and reached for it.

"Oh, now we're *grabby* Gabby," Roderick laughed at her, but he cut off a corner of his calzone and put it aside to cool. "Not yet," he said. "Hot, hot, hot!" He signed it with his free hand and Gabby imitated him, spitting blueberry as she blew into her clawed hand. "Ha! Ha! Ha!" she mimicked, then she cackled and squashed a garbanzo bean on her tray.

By the end of their meal, Gabby looked like a slayer of Smurfs and there was a radius of purple-blue-stained chickpea rejects on the floor around her chair. The corner of the calzone that she had been greedy for was met with disdain and Roderick had ended up eating it after all, stained violet from Gabby's fingers.

He left the high chair tray in the sink, slipped his phone back into his pocket, and carried Gabby straight to the bathroom for a bath. Once he had put her down in the tub with her favorite toys and a few inches of warm water, carefully checked for temperature on the inside of his elbow, he settled back on his heels and watched her. She was strong enough to sit up reliably in the tub now and loved the splashing. They played peekaboo until she got bored with him and scooted to entertain herself with the floating toys.

Roderick found himself fingering the phone in his pocket. Addison. She wasn't just pretty but smoking hot. He wanted to call her so badly, just to hear her voice again. Surely, it wouldn't hurt to see how she'd put herself into his contacts.

He sat on the toilet, keeping Gabby firmly in his sights, and unlocked the phone. Addison Carmichael, she'd put in, and then in the notes: (Teacher Addy).

And there was her number.

Roderick looked at it hungrily, and Gabby chose that

moment to yell in triumph or frustration (it was hard to tell which) and bring a plastic shark down into the water hard enough to splash outside of the tub towards him. He jerked the phone to the side to save it from the water and put it on the counter as he rose to his feet. "Hey sweetie, let's not do that to your poor shark. Let's get the rest of your blueberries off and call it a night, okay?"

Gabby protested her extraction from the tub with a heart-broken wail, until he had her standing on her feet and wrapped in a towel and was playing peekaboo with her around the terrycloth.

Then, from the counter came a tiny voice. "Hello? Roderick? Are you there?"

He had accidentally dialed Addison.

9

It wasn't that Addison was right next to her phone waiting for Roderick to call like a teenage girl with a crush, not really.

She just happened to be gazing wistfully at the lock screen when he called, that was all. Like she'd been gazing at it every five minutes since she arrived home at her cousin's crowded little house.

"Hello?" she said at once.

Distantly, a voice said, "—poor shark! Let's (something) blueberries (something) call it a night."

Then there was splashing and a shrieking protest that Addy knew entirely too well, which swiftly gave way to giggles and the sound of a peekaboo game. "Who's a wet little girl?" Roderick asked. "Who's going to be dry?"

Addison felt like an eavesdropper, realizing at once that Roderick must have accidentally dialed her number. She was overhearing an adorable moment between father and daughter, and it would be creepy for her to continue in silence.

"Hello?" she said cautiously. "Roderick? Are you there?"

"Shi—shoot!" came Roderick's far-off voice, then the

sound of a phone fumbling. Then he was at the other end of the line in earnest, his voice sounding so close and warm that it sent shivers down Addison's spine. "I didn't mean to call you! I mean, not yet. I was going to call after I got Gabby down, I must've dialed when I fumbled the phone. I'm so sorry. Oh my God, I'm a dolt."

"It's okay," Addison was quick to reply sincerely. "That sounded like quite a struggle."

"There was a shark involved," Roderick said, sounding further away again. "Don't eat the towel, Gabby. It's not tasty."

"Ababa ababa!" Gabby replied. "Yuck! Yuck!"

"Yuck!" Roderick agreed, absolutely melting Addison. "Are you ready for a bedtime story? Who wants a book? Who wants a hungry, hungry caterpillar?"

Gabby's response was confused; Addison guessed that she knew it was a trap to get her into bed and she giggled.

"I could call you back," Roderick offered, his voice all hers again, but Addison thought he sounded reluctant.

"But then I wouldn't get to hear The Very Hungry Cater-pillar," Addison protested.

It was ridiculous to think that she could hear him smile.

He put her on speakerphone and Gabby must have leaned very close because her voice was very loud as she said solemnly, "Gabby addy!"

Just nonsense noises, Addison reminded herself, but she couldn't quite keep the warm feeling of inclusion from spreading across her chest.

Getting Gabby into a clean diaper and dressed for bed sounded like another battle for the history books. Roderick gave it a sports play-by-play for Addison's amusement. "There's a leg in the romper! Score one for the dad! Whoops, there goes an arm! Score for the baby! No, no wiggling away! The penalty is tickling!"

At the final snap of the romper, he must have lifted her into the air, because Gabby gave a squeal of delight. There was a weird moment and a creak of a chair, then Gabby's breath sounded very near the phone as Roderick began to read.

Addison was in Wendy's over-crowded sewing room, lying back on the inflatable mattress, half under a table, surrounded by storage boxes. Some of them were her cousin's and some of them were her own. She closed her eyes and imagined Roderick with Gabby in the crook of his arm. His big, well-muscled arm, covered in soft brown skin. His long, clever fingers, turning the pages of the book. His beautiful mouth, his white teeth.

Was he *trying* to make The Very Hungry Caterpillar sound sexy? Addison had not guessed it was possible, but the low, easy tone of his voice reading, "On Saturday, he ate through one piece of chocolate cake, one ice-cream cone, one pickle..." set her blood on fire.

She wanted to be that ice-cream cone.

This wasn't *instinct*, she chided herself. This was just general desperation faced with the most gorgeous guy she'd ever met. Didn't she know better by now than to let herself get swept up in intense feelings?

Her lynx had other ideas, convinced beyond everything logical that this was the compass direction of their ultimate happiness.

"Are you sleepy?" Roderick asked.

"No," Addison said before she realized he was speaking to Gabby. She flushed, glad Roderick couldn't see her cheeks color.

Gabby made a grumpy sound that Addison recognized as fighting sleep. "Buh! Buh!"

"You want another book?" Roderick offered.

"Buh," Gabby insisted.

"Good Night, Good Night Construction Site?" The book must have been in reach because Roderick began reading it at once.

Gabby was snoring lightly by the end of that book. "Hang on," Roderick whispered, and there was the clink of the phone onto a table, the creak of the chair, and the rustle of blankets.

Gabby woke up as he lay her down and cried disconsolately as the phone was suddenly muffled in a hand and a door clicked behind him.

The toddler sobbed for just a moment, then went quiet. "That's always the worst," Roderick confessed quietly into the phone. He must have taken it off speakerphone because it sounded like he was right next to her.

"You're an amazing dad," Addison said softly in return. Questions crowded into her mind. Who was Gabby's mother? Was she still in their life? Would Addison ever be a part of that life?

They were silent a long moment, then both said, "So…" at the same time.

"Tell me about you," Roderick said first. "Where are you from? How did you come to Nickel City?"

Initially, Addison felt awkward talking about herself, but before she knew it, she was telling him about growing up in Kansas, moving to Buffalo in New York—she skipped the time in California—taking a job as a nanny, getting her degree in early education. "I didn't want to stay in the city," she said. "As soon as the kids aged out of me, I got my education certificate and started looking around for somewhere to live that wasn't so crowded, a place I could shift, maybe."

"What are—no, I'm sorry, it's rude."

"I'm a lynx," Addison offered shyly. "Canadian lynx. I wanted someplace quiet, someplace that got snow once in a while. A couple of months ago, my cousin, Wendy, told me about her friend who was looking to open a shifters-only day care and it sounded perfect."

"Wendy who runs the DMV?" Roderick guessed.

"That's the one," Addison said with a wince. Wendy could come on strong; did she have a good reputation in town, or had she made enemies here?

"Gabby likes her," Roderick said as if that was clearly good enough for him. "Are you guys close?"

"We were both kids in Kansas together," Addison explained. "She used to drag me into all kinds of trouble. But I hadn't seen her in years before I moved out here to work for Cherry."

"Are you planning to stay with her long?"

Addison chewed on her lip. "No, her house is really small, so I'm looking for a place. You don't happen to know anyone looking for a roommate, do you? I was looking at local rentals, but they're sky high. I didn't expect New York prices here."

"I have a spare room," Roderick said unexpectedly, and they were both silent for a moment.

Addison made herself chuckle when he did, but it was more from horror than humor.

She had made the mistake of moving right in with her last boyfriend, Owen. It had been convenient, at first, there was no reason for her to have her own place when Owen had the extra space and needed her, at least emotionally. He had a car and a credit card, too, and discouraged her from getting either. She never had any utilities in her own name, no credit, and it had trapped her in what had become a loveless power trip of a relationship for entirely too long.

Addison had to close her eyes and sort out what she was feeling; it was hard to feel her instinct through the guilt and anger she still carried, just as it had been hard to feel it over her sympathy and attraction for Owen.

She had craved love so badly that pity and chemistry overwhelmed the little tickle of her lynx's intuition. She wanted to believe that she was smarter now, that her instinct was stronger and her common sense more honed, but was that really true? How much of this dizzy certainty was just her loneliness and longing for family, her physical response to an inviting smile and a handsome face? Not to mention that amazing physique.

Instinct wasn't warning her now, it was a warm flush of encouragement, but she'd already spent years of her life recovering from her own impulsive actions.

"That wouldn't really be..." Addy said, just as Roderick said, "That's probably not a good idea."

"I appreciate the offer," Addison added shyly. "It's just..."

"...A little fast," Roderick agreed swiftly.

The whole thing felt absurdly fast, even though they hadn't even kissed. Every time she talked to him, every glimpse of him, every overheard moment with Gabby, Addison could feel herself falling harder.

But she barely knew the guy. She didn't know what music he liked, or what books, beyond The Very Hungry Caterpillar.

She had gotten burned moving way too fast with Owen.

Instinct told her this was different, but...instinct wasn't enough.

10

*R*oderick had never been big on phones. They were useful for work, and it was nice being able to snap a quick photo of Gabby, but the idea of conversing with someone for fun was completely alien. Calls were completed as quickly as possible.

Until Addison.

He sat down on the couch with the phone against his ear and eagerly listened for every word and telltale intake of breath.

Endorphins, he decided. There was a logical explanation for why talking to her felt so rewarding, and it didn't have anything to do with *instinct,* only brain chemicals. He'd been alone so long that the idea of romance was just kicking lots of hormones and neurotransmitters loose or something.

His wolf had very different ideas, absolutely sure that Addison was simply equivalent to happiness. Explaining how chemistry and biology worked to his wolf had always been challenging. To his canine companion, everything was something to fight, to flee, or to claim, and why didn't matter.

"I think it's your turn," Addison said, once they had laughingly acknowledged that moving in together was simply absurd.

It took Roderick a moment to set aside the gorgeous fantasy of having her at his side every night, getting Gabby down together, retiring to... "My...uh...turn?"

"I told you about growing up in Kansas. Where did you grow up?"

Roderick told her about the little town in the south where he'd lived until he was ten, his parent's divorce, moving to Nickel City with his mother, and her subsequent death a few years before Gabby's birth. "She would have liked you," he told Addy.

*Who **wouldn't** like her?* his wolf wanted to know. Roderick was beginning to think that his wolf liked Addison better than he liked Roderick.

Obviously, his wolf teased.

Thanks, Roderick replied.

"I'm sorry you lost her," Addison said sympathetically. "My dad died when I was in school, so I know how hard it is."

They talked about weathering grief and their coping methods. "I got mad at first," Roderick confessed. "Because it wasn't fair, you know. I made terrible decisions." He was shocked by how easy it was to say so out loud. Was it because of the facelessness of the phone, that it was less painful to confess things? Or was it because every sense in his body told him that Addison was *safe,* the way no one had ever been *safe* before?

"I got myself an awful boyfriend," Addison sympathized. "I quit school for an unhealthy relationship with a guy who didn't let me control my own money or drive a car."

Roderick tried to squelch his rage. "Who is he? Can I pound him for you?"

Addison laughed softly. "Owen is long gone. I had to dodge a private investigator and move across the country to get work under the table, but I was lucky enough to get out of it with a great job as a nanny and I never looked back. I haven't heard from him in years now."

Roderick hoped he never met this Owen character, because he wasn't sure he'd be able to restrain himself in the face of someone who had treated Addison so poorly.

They talked for a little while about college—Roderick had gotten a degree in art at the community college before taking an apprenticeship with the plumbing union.

"You're an artist?" Addison said in awe. "You'll have to show me some of your work!"

Roderick thought ruefully of his college assignments and the sketchbooks he hadn't picked up in months. "I don't have much. I loved the *idea* of doing art much more than I actually loved doing the art."

Addison commiserated. "I thought I might be a writer, for a while. I only got about four chapters in before I realized exactly how hard it was. My story went completely off the rails and I hated all my characters."

"Sounds like a best seller to me," Roderick teased.

It was easy to talk with her, picturing her expressions, remembering her shy, wiggly fingered wave when he picked Gabby up. He felt like he was sloshing with emotion, like his heart was full of anticipation and longing.

And then Addison reluctantly asked the question they had both clearly been dreading, "Who was Gabby's mom?"

To Roderick's surprise, it wasn't hard to explain. "Dana is an ad executive, and Nickel City was just a quick stop-over for her, a job on the way to the top. We...had a whirlwind romance and weren't careful. A big opportunity for her came up just as we found out about Gabby. Dana made it clear that her job was more important than a baby and wanted to give her up. I couldn't do that. So I chose Gabby, and she chose her career. It was...pretty much an amicable split, and I think we both feel like we got the better end of the deal. She got her freedom, I got a drooly little tyrant that I adore." He didn't mention instinct.

Addison was quiet for a moment and Roderick had a split-second fear that he'd said too much, been too raw. They really were moving too fast, and he'd just over-shared in a big way.

"Gabby's a lucky girl," Addison said warmly. "Are you...worried that Dana would ever come back for her?"

"I think that Dana was more worried that I'd come after her for child support or try to dump Gabby on her. She had a lawyer draw up papers and I have full custody, free and clear. Well, not free. My lord, diapers are expensive, and I nearly had a heart attack looking at the prices for college."

At the other end of the line there was a distant knock and the muffled cadence of a voice.

"I'm good, thanks," Addison called, away from the receiver. "I'm on the phone!"

The far-off voice sounded apologetic and Addison was back, "Sorry. Wendy was just offering a nightcap."

There was a moment of quiet on the line and Roderick wished he could see her face and try to read the emotions there.

Her voice was quiet. "So, do you think this is...? Do you feel...?"

"...Instinct?" Roderick guessed when she trailed off.

Her exhale was faint through the phone. "*Instinct.* Is this just...? I mean I like you, and I think that we could have something, but...?"

"My mother had lots of opinions about instinct and mates," Roderick said carefully. "And I've always believed that the magic of being a shifter gives me certain advantages."

"You don't think that the whole idea of mates is absurd?"

"I used to..." Roderick told her, and the air between them

was so charged that he imagined he could feel her breath when she exhaled on the phone. He desperately wished that she was there, on the couch with him. But he also knew that it would be impossible to *resist* her if she was.

"What do we do from here?" Addison asked hesitantly.

"I've got that spare bedroom..." Roderick offered teasingly, then quickly added, "I'm kidding, I'm only kidding. That would be insane."

She laughed weakly. "Right, let's just move in together the day after we meet. That's sensible."

"My dear deceased mother would rise from the grave and beat some better sense into me," Roderick chuckled. "But I would like to take you out some time, and just...see where this goes. Can I take you out to lunch? Tomorrow?"

Addison paused. "Cherry mentioned that she had someone else part time who would be coming in tom—"

Roderick listened intently for several heartbeats before he realized that his phone had gone dead.

11

Addison groaned and fell back on her mattress when the phone disconnected. She guessed his phone had run out of charge; they'd talked for more than an hour, and her own phone was protesting with a red battery warning.

Roderick.

He was gorgeous and funny and she was already head-over-heels for him. She hadn't been this nervous and excited about a guy since...well, since Owen.

Was this the same thing? A silly crush on someone she barely knew, willing to move way too fast because of intense feelings?

Just look where that had gotten her before.

But this time, her lynx was purring in her chest, happy and satisfied, sure of their fate. Addison had been willing to overlook her lynx's reservations before; their roles were almost reversed now. She was determined not to get swept up in anything too fast again.

It was just that when they spoke, when she saw him, everything seemed simple and safe.

Addison held her phone up above her and stared at the list of recent calls, then went in and added Roderick's name to her contacts. She considered giving him a special ringtone, then decided that was entirely too much.

She rolled to her feet and wandered out to find Wendy standing tip-toe on a step stool, pulling a box from the top of a cabinet.

Wendy loved projects. Sewing, knitting, crocheting, making dolls, sculpting...her entire house was filled with haphazardly labeled boxes full of supplies. "Oh, there you are!" she said cheerfully when Addison came into the kitchen. "I was beginning to wonder if you'd just gone to bed."

"No, I was talking on the phone." To *Roderick.* It was like having Pop Rocks in her chest, every time she thought of him.

"Did you find a place to rent?" Wendy asked, skipping down the stool with her arms loaded. "I mean, not that I'm trying to kick you out that soon. You're welcome to stay as long as you want."

Roderick had a spare room, Addison thought, and every time she remembered, her heart did a curious little flip, because she loved the idea of moving in with him, even as she cautioned herself that she'd never be able to resist him at that proximity and they were already moving at crazy speeds.

"No," she said reluctantly. "I'm looking, but most of the places around here are way, way out of my price range."

"I got an offer for my house in the mail today!" Wendy said. "'We're buying property in your neighborhood! Contact us for an offer well above appraisal!'" She plopped the box down on the table and opened the lid to riffle through what looked like leather scraps.

"Well, that doesn't sound shady at all," Addison scoffed.

"I didn't realize I'd be encouraging you to move here in the middle of a housing bubble," Wendy said apologetically as she found the exact scrap she'd been searching for and held it up triumphantly.

"Oh, don't worry about it," Addison assured her. "I already love it here. I can probably find some way to weather it until the bubble bursts. Some way that isn't hopelessly underfoot. There are some apartments in the warehouse district I could probably afford..."

"I am not letting you move to The Tails," Wendy was quick to interrupt. She scrambled back up the step stool with the box.

"The Tails?"

"It's a play on the nickel in Nickel City, heads or tails," Wendy explained as she wedged the box back into the space it had miraculously come out of. "The Tails are full of crime and poverty. Bad side of the tracks, if you will."

"I didn't realize Nickel City had anything like that," Addison said. "It looks so pretty and idyllic. There are so many trees."

"It's a nice place," Wendy agreed. "It feels good when you come here, but even really pretty apples might have a few bruises."

Addison's phone gave a buzz then, and she had a thrill of anticipation as she saw a text from Roderick on the screen and turned away to read it.

Sorry battery went dead. Would lunch tomorrow work?

Addison tapped in a reply. *I hope so. I'll confirm with Cherry in the morning.* Then she spent entirely too much time staring at the screen hoping for a reply.

"Who was that?" Wendy asked slyly as she turned back. "You're blushing."

Great! came the answer on her phone.

She didn't need to respond, Addison told herself, so she refrained from answering in a string of hearts or something else she would regret later. "Just a...guy. The dad of one of the kids at the day care."

"Ooooooo," Wendy said knowingly. "Is it *instinct?*"

Wendy wasn't a shifter, but she'd grown up with them, and she'd always given Addison a pale imitation of shifter recognition, a little warning tingle like a child who might start shifting soon...but she'd never actually manifested an animal counterpart.

Addison tried to brush it off. "I don't know," she lied as her lynx protested. "Probably it's nothing. He's just...asked me to lunch tomorrow."

"An hour on the phone the night you meet and a lunch date in the middle of your second day of work. Probably it's nothing," Wendy mocked her. "Addy has a ma-ate! Addy has a ma-ate!"

It was just the sort of ribbing that she would have done when they were kids together and Addison, still blushing, laughed and snapped towards her with a dishtowel.

"We're taking it slow," Addison insisted. "There's no reason to rush." She thought about Roderick's spare room rather wistfully.

"Well, good luck on your date," Wendy said kindly.

"Thanks," Addison said sheepishly. "It's just lunch..."

Wendy made a noise of disbelief. "Go on believing that, then." She bent to whatever she was in the middle of crafting on her kitchen table—it involved a hot glue gun, string, and feathers, as well as the leather scrap she'd found. She whispered, "Addy has a ma-ate, Addy has ma-ate."

Addy brushed her teeth, balancing her bathroom kit carefully on the ledge of the sink, and went back to her mattress in the sewing room. She changed into pajamas and cuddled down under one of Wendy's quilts.

She lay awake replaying The Very Hungry Caterpillar in her mind and was desperately hungry for all sorts of things that weren't food at all.

12

Addison was every bit as adorable as Roderick remembered and he stood, craning to look over the gate at her for a long moment before she glanced around and saw them.

"Good morning, Gabby!" she greeted him cheerfully.

Gabby recognized at that moment that she was going to be left behind and buried her face in Roderick's collarbone with a cry of alarm.

"Oh, no!" Addison said lightly as she came to the gate. "Am I the big bad wolf this morning?"

Gabby peeked back at her, trying to decide if she was a threat.

"Grrr," Addison teased, and she made finger claws.

Gabby giggled, but she didn't offer to ease her death-grip on Roderick's shirt.

"Oh, shoes," Roderick remembered. "Not that she's walking on them yet."

"She's pretty close, though," Addison observed. "She's pulling up and she'll walk a little holding my hands."

Gabby was uncooperative about letting him remove her

tennis shoes, but he managed to get them off of her feet and replace them with the elastic leather slippers that keep her socks on her feet for most of the day.

There were four unmatched socks pinned to the board that morning. Roderick was pretty sure at least one of them was Gabby's but would have been hard-pressed to pick out which one. Most mornings, he figured he was lucky to get two socks on her at all and he was glad to get her home with all her fingers and toes.

"I'm not sure if I'm actually looking forward to her walking or not," Roderick confessed. "It's going to take chasing her to a whole new level of difficulty."

Addison laughed and nodded. "Believe me, I know!"

There was a shy moment and Roderick finally dredged up the courage to ask, "About lunch...?"

"I can join you if you don't mind a late lunch," Addison said, just as bashfully. "The kids have a quiet time right after lunch and Shea will be here. I've got an hour break scheduled."

"That sounds perfect," Roderick said genuinely.

"Cherry promised it would be no trouble. And she got me to fill out a W2, so I think we're serious about this job now!"

Relief flooded Roderick. Addison was *staying*. She was staying in Nickel City and he wouldn't lose her any time soon. He hadn't even realized that he was worried about it until he wasn't.

"Great!" he said enthusiastically. "Great!" He was like a puppy, he thought, all but drooling on her feet.

"Ready to play some games, Gabby?" Addison asked.

Gabby looked between the two of them and her face crumpled.

"I'll be back before you know it," Roderick promised her.

Their handoff meant that they brushed arms, and it was

everything that Roderick could do not to kiss her when their faces were unexpectedly close.

Gabby cried in earnest as he left, and Roderick could hear Addison saying soothingly, "It's okay, I know, I know," as she bounced the toddler in her arms. "It's so hard being little."

He drove a little way out of town for his next job, taking a winding way along through quiet neighborhoods. There were a lot of pending sales on houses, and he saw no less than three rental cars in front of places with cute names above their doors.

He only realized about halfway to his destination that he'd been unconsciously looking for houses for rent.

It was ridiculous and out of bounds to be looking for a place for a woman he'd just met to live, he scolded himself.

His wolf was just confused about why Addison wouldn't immediately come live with them, where she belonged.

13

Addison blushed when Cherry caught her checking her phone for new texts for the fifth time and reminded herself firmly that it was only her second day of work and she ought to be more focused.

She put her phone up out of reach in the teacher's office so she wouldn't be tempted to keep checking it, then sat with the kids to help the youngest with the craft they were making that day, involving paper plates and dry noodles.

Tara helped her keep the littlest ones from trying to eat their supplies and gave Addison shy, hopeful smiles when Addison praised her.

Gabby spit out her noodle. "Yuck! Yuck!"

Each of the kids who was shifting had a sticker by their name at the cubbies that showed their animal. It was an easy way to share the information in a way that was non-incriminating if there were human visitors. While grown-ups might not volunteer what kind of shifter they were to each other, it was important to know what the kids were capable of, and what to look for if one went missing!

Addison wasn't sure where Cherry had found an

armadillo sticker, but most surprising was the sticker next to Tara's cubby—a delicate white unicorn.

She spent the morning focussing on that puzzle rather than thinking about Roderick or wrestling her doubts. "Why does Tara think her shift form is ugly?" she asked Cherry quietly when there was a brief gap in games, diapers, books, and keeping Amy from hitting other kids exuberantly with trains. They were sitting together on one of the benches letting the kids doctor them, which at this moment involved a great deal of consultation on the far side of the rabbit cage.

Cherry seemed surprised and frowned thoughtfully. "She does? She's a new enrollment, and I thought she just needed some extra time to get comfortable. They are new, and I think her mother is having a hard time. Did Tara say that to you? That she was *ugly?*"

Addison might have been pleased with Tara's trust, but she was more concerned with Tara's self-image. "Is she really a unicorn?" Addison knew that there were rare mythical shifters, but she'd never met one. "Have you ever seen her shift?"

"That's what her mother said," Cherry said. "But I've never actually seen her change. I just assumed that she wasn't sure we were safe yet, kids that age have heard lots of warnings not to shift in front of strangers and Tara is a cautious girl. Thank you for mentioning it, I'll talk to her." Then she regarded Addison more carefully. "Or you can. She seems to trust you. Can you get her to show you her form? Maybe there's something we can help with."

Addison slowly smiled back. "I'd be glad to try."

Then Cherry laughed in unexpected relief. "I'm so happy to have you here, Addison. I really am glad that Wendy suggested you, and I hope you'll stick around Nickel City." She slung an arm around Addison and gave her shoulders a warm squeeze. "My instinct tells me you're a keeper."

Addison gave her a sideways look of surprise. "Do you have instinct?" she asked in astonishment.

"Maybe not your shifter sparkly magic instinct," Cherry scoffed. "But I can get a good read of a person by how they act around children, and how kids react in return. Call it common sense or just experience, but I know a good person when I meet one, and you're the right stuff. I'm happy to have you on board and I know you'll fit in here in Nickel City."

Addison felt a wave of gratitude and pleasure wash over her and realized that she'd been desperately hoping for the praise but not expecting it. "Thank you," she said shyly. "I already love it here."

Then someone at the far side of the rabbit cage gave a cry of outrage and what had been a good-natured discussion turned into Gil shedding his clothing to turn into an armadillo as two of the older kids started shoving each other.

"No, thank you!" Cherry said firmly as she sprang to her feet and went to intercept them. "No thank you for touches that your friend doesn't want!"

She deftly got them all untangled and into line to wash their hands for lunch, which was like trying to thread a frayed shoelace into a hole that was too small on the best of days.

Addison watched the clock through lunch with the same eagerness she had been watching her phone for texts, counting down the minutes to lunch, and then naptime, and her *date*.

But lunch went swiftly sideways.

Gil unscrewed his water bottle to peer inside of it for no good reason and Robert knocked it over trying to fence with his cheese stick. As Addison grabbed paper towels to soak up the water, Amy swept her entire lunch off of her tray and cackled in triumph. Gabby less successfully tried to do the same, managing only to smear her food all over her sleeves.

Gil was shouting, Robert was protesting his innocence, Amy had realized that none of her food was in reach anymore and was crying, Gabby was just making noise to play along, and Tara was trying to sink into her chair...when one of the babies woke up and began to wail.

Addison tried to calm the boys and glanced at the clock in consternation as Cherry went to check on the baby. Roderick would be there any moment and she couldn't possibly leave with the day care in chaos like this.

"It's just water, Gil," she said, as soothingly as she could. "We'll refill your bottle just as soon as we clean this up! Robert, can you help your friend?"

"Gil wasn't supposed to open his bottle!" Robert said defensively. "It's not my fault!" He was gathering his lunch back out of the way of the spreading puddle.

"No one is saying it's your fault, Robert," Addison said, forcing herself to be patient. "I'd just like you to help clean it up. There are paper towels on the counter. Just a few at a time—!" She knew that the boys had a habit of grabbing off as many as they could, using dozens of squares for small jobs.

Amy was screeching at the top of her lungs now and Gabby clearly thought it was a competition. The second baby woke with a whimper and broke into a squall of consternation.

The front door of the day care gave a chime of warning and Addison scrambled for her phone to check the camera before one of the kids could shift out of sheer emotional reaction.

"That's Shea," Cherry called from the nursery area. "What excellent timing!"

Addison felt a curious calm settle over her at the sight of the woman who came in. She was a short, middle-aged

Japanese woman with slate gray hair in a shoulder-length cut, and her eyes crinkled in amusement when she looked up at Addison.

Addison's anxiousness eased. Everyone in the room seemed to take a breath at the same moment and, although Amy resumed crying, it was with a fraction of her previous zest.

"I'm Addison," she said. She almost yawned, she felt so relaxed.

"Shea!" They shook hands and Addison smiled at her bemusedly.

The effect seemed to ease when Shea floated back into the nursery area and scooped up the second baby, who was only panting now and settled immediately upon being picked up.

Robert had indeed wadded up half the roll of paper towels to clean up the water, but Addison found that she didn't feel the slightest bit cross about it. She only laughed and helped everyone pick up their lunch bags as they finished and got up to wipe their mats down. Amy was re-stocked with cheese cubes and crackers and Gabby licked her squashed blueberries from her arms.

Then Addison's lynx gave a little shiver of happy anticipation and she heard the buzz of the front door.

14

$\mathcal{R}$oderick would have jumped the gate to meet Addison if getting his boots off wasn't such a pain in the butt. They were solid work boots, with laces, so he stuck to the parent side of the gate out of respect for Cherry's no-shoes rule. He noticed on his way in that there were now six socks pinned to the "'BEAR' FEET" sign. Only two of them matched.

Addison appeared at the gate and stepped nimbly over, then seemed to hesitate.

She was smiling, but shy, and Roderick knew that he must look foolish, grinning like a loon right back at her.

"Hi," she said, coming to stand right in front of him. "My shoes are behind you."

"Oops!" Roderick chuckled and moved aside so that she could sit and pull a pair of practical tennis shoes out from underneath the bench.

He was still wearing his plain work clothes, and she was dressed in clothing appropriate to a day care; they had both considered this an informal lunch and Roderick was glad to find that their expectations had aligned.

When she had finished tying her shoes, Addison bounced to her feet. "Do you have a place in mind for lunch?"

"Do you mind walking a block?" Roderick asked. "I thought I'd take you to Heads Up Cafe. It's a little bakery that does great lunches. We should be there just after the main lunch rush and there are places to sit on the porch."

"I'd like that," Addison said, and they stood for a moment, smiling at each other. Roderick finally opened the door for her and wondered if it would be too forward to take her hand. He decided it would, and they spent a little awkward time figuring out how far apart to walk, how fast to stride, and how much to glance at each other as they went.

"Nickel City is so pretty," Addison said, as they had to walk closer together around a tree that dominated the sidewalk. "I know that Montana was supposed to be beautiful, but the photos don't even do it justice. All the mountains and forests, it's like being in a postcard."

"Have you been up to the overlook of Belle Lake?" Roderick asked, trying to decide if he should give her more space now that they were past the tree. He didn't really want to.

Addison shook her head. "No, I went to see the famous big tree out that way, but I didn't make it to either the shore of the lake or the overlook."

"It's worth a trip," Roderick assured her. "Sunset is pretty amazing there." He didn't add that it was a popular make-out spot among young locals, or fill her in on the other uncommon features of the forest; some things weren't topics for first not-dates like this, especially in public.

Heads Up Cafe was busier than he'd hoped, but they chatted as they stood in line, picking up where they'd left off from their phone call with the same easy friendliness that left him warm to his toes. They talked about Nickel City, and how it stacked up to Buffalo, Gabby and her love of blueberries, favorite foods, and how tastes changed.

"I used to hate olives," Addison said, "but I can't get enough of them now. I love a pizza covered with nothing but olives and cheese."

"I used to go by the name Rod," Roderick said with a grimace. "I thought it was clever."

"It's a bold nickname," Addison agreed, blushing and laughing.

"I decided it would interfere with my business aspirations. Who's going to take their plumber seriously with a name like Rod?"

Addison giggled. "I don't know, maybe it's got some truth in advertising, depending on the tools you use."

Roderick wasn't sure how she could look so innocent and still sound so dirty.

"I fear that I've doomed my daughter to the same kind of shame," he confessed. "But Gabriella seemed like too much of a mouthful for a baby, so it just sort of evolved to Gabby."

"It's a beautiful name! You'll have to hold it in reserve," Addison advised. "Full names for when she's in big trouble."

They got to the counter and there was only the briefest moment of hesitation before Addison placed her order and paid, not offering to split a ticket with Roderick. He ordered a club sandwich, and they took their table number and threaded their way through the people who were waiting for their takeout.

There was a couple just leaving a prime table on the porch and Roderick stepped in and claimed it while Addison got napkins and water glasses. He made sure that she got the seat with a view of the mountains.

They skirted the topic of politics carefully enough to establish that they had the same basic leanings and lingered over more fun topics, like favorite Beatles, and worst fashion mistakes from high school (sagging pants for him, ripped up jeans with lots of safety pins for her).

"Not again," Addison vowed.

"We'll never speak of it," Roderick promised.

Just as Roderick was starting to be convinced that their sandwich order had been forgotten or accidentally taken by a careless tourist, a harried waitress brought their plates and dropped them on the table in front of them.

"Thank you!" Addison said sincerely. "Oh, Rod, you weren't kidding. This looks amazing!"

Roderick groaned. "I'm going to regret telling you that name, aren't I."

Her eyes were crinkled with amusement and she must have read on his face that he wasn't really bothered. "I promise to use it only for powers of good."

Everything about her was good, Roderick thought, biting into his giant sandwich ravenously. He would have guessed she worked with children even if he hadn't met her at the day care; she had a quiet, relentlessly cheerful manner that suited handling pets and kids.

They talked more as they ate, about heavier subjects like loss and regret. Roderick coaxed a little more of the story of her last boyfriend from her, a tale that made him clench a fist in his lap because that Owen character had clearly preyed on her naivety and youth.

"You know the type," Addison said, deliberately off-handed. "Or, maybe you don't. The kind that seems just fine at first, just a little...needy. Flattering courtship with fancy dinners that he never let you pay for. And then it's been six months and you realize that he's gaslighted you away from having any friends that aren't his and emotionally manipulated you into not having any life or means of your own. I didn't have a car or credit or contacts or financial stability to be on my own..."

"I'd still deck him for you," Roderick offered.

"It's been years since I heard from him." Addison's look was complicated: thoughtful and grateful and a little afraid.

Understandably so.

Instinct was whispering again, warning him. If he pushed too hard, asked too much too quickly, she would run. Underneath that sunny smile and cheerful resilience, she'd been hurt. She'd given her trust too soon before, and Roderick didn't want to give her any reason to doubt his sincerity. He could be patient; his wolf suggested that it would be worth a slow courtship to win this woman.

"I have a date on Friday," he said, as off-handedly as he could manage.

Addison froze and Roderick could see her turning over that information, trying to decide what he meant by it.

"You'd be welcome to join us," Roderick added quickly, fearing the joke was too weak. "Gabby's not the jealous type."

Addison's face split into a laughing smile. "Are you asking me on a date?"

"Does it count as a date at a restaurant where you can color your own menu, with a fourteen-month-old chaperone?" Roderick asked.

"I don't know," Addison said, pretending to think about it. "Does this count as a date?"

Did it? Separate tickets, a simple sandwich? "Do I get a kiss at the end?" As soon as he said the words, Roderick wondered if it was exactly what he'd just warned himself not to do.

Addison gazed at him, her lips just slightly parted, like she was ready to say something but wasn't sure what.

"No pressure," he said quickly. "They are *your* lips."

The lips in question curved up at the corners. "Indeed," she said demurely. "And these lips need to get back to Cherry's by two-thirty."

They hastily bussed their dishes, and Roderick was glad that they fell right back into a comfortable conversation that carried them all the way back to the day care. There were seven socks on the "'BEAR' FEET" sign now.

Addison sat down to take off her tennis shoes and Roderick tried not to tower over her. "I had a really nice time," he said gruffly. "Thank you for joining me."

She smiled up at him like sunshine. "I had a great time," she agreed. "And I'd love to go out to dinner with you and your fourteen-month-old chaperone on Friday."

Roderick's heart leaped in his chest. "I'll pick you up at six?"

Addison cocked her head. "Why don't I meet you there," she counter-proposed.

Roderick extended his hand, and she shook it with a surprisingly strong grip. "Sounds great," he said sincerely.

Then there was the sound of something falling in the playroom behind him and there was the wail of an outraged child that might have been his own.

"I'm back to work!" Addison said, springing to her stocking feet. "Thank you!"

15

*N*ickel City felt like nowhere else that Addison had ever been, and she was pretty sure that it wasn't just that it felt like she'd come here to meet her soulmate. The air seemed to reach further down into her lungs. Her lynx was stronger here, her senses sharper. She had a brief chance to shift and play with the kids in the backyard of the day care that Cherry still hadn't settled on a name for and even shifting felt easier; she hardly had to think about it to flow into her lynx form.

Everything felt alive, full of magic and energy.

She'd never seen so many shifters in one place before, either. She ran into them unexpectedly—shopping in grocery stores, behind the counter of the bakery, jogging through the forest park in the middle of town—instead of just at the day care where she might expect them. It was no wonder they needed an actual establishment for shifter child care here.

There were plenty of humans in the little town as well, of course. But where she might sense another shifter once or twice a week in the bustling city of Buffalo, here, she ran into them half a dozen times in just her first few days.

They always gave each other friendly nods of recognition, a grin, and a little tip up of the chin in greeting, and Addison felt like she belonged, like she'd come home, and her instinct said *here. Now.*

The surrounding humans weren't completely oblivious to the silent camaraderie, Addison thought, and she sometimes caught one of them giving a suspicious look after an unspoken greeting. She wondered if it didn't look a little cliquish, and she was more surreptitious in her acknowledgments after that.

Everything about Nickel City would be perfect if it weren't for the fact that she was living in Wendy's sewing room.

It wasn't that Wendy was a bad housemate—she didn't have unreasonable expectations on Addison's time or eat her food in the refrigerator. But it wasn't a lot of house to share, and Addison was very aware that it wasn't her space.

"Do you want me to bring back a sandwich?" Addison offered from the bathroom. She was attempting to tame her curly hair with a broad curling iron, an act severely hampered by the fact that there was no free surface in the bathroom to put the hot device down on. She had to fuss with each lock of hair one at a time, without a free hand to brush it loose. It was a laborious process, and Addison was not at all sure it was worth the time she was spending on it.

"No, you don't have to do that!" Wendy called from the living room. She was making...something...on a mannequin in front of the television. It seemed to involve a lot of sheer draped cloth and a whole lot of pins, but Addison wasn't ready to guess what it might be. "You're going on a *date!*"

"It's not really a date!" Addison protested. "I don't think you can call it a date when you're going with a fourteen-month-old and her dad. It's just a...dinner. At a family restaurant." With *Roderick.* "I really don't mind bringing you home a sandwich!"

She snatched the iron away from the ear she'd gotten it too close to and swore as Wendy said something. "Sorry, I didn't hear that?"

"I said this needs embroidered ribbon! I think I have some in your room."

But it wasn't Addison's room. It was the sewing room, and she was living out of a few suitcases. Her car was still full of all her moving boxes except the one she'd unpacked to find her curling iron. Did she have to have so much hair? Her arms were not used to this much primping, and muscles that she didn't usually use were starting to burn from holding them up so long.

"Go on in," Addison said. Wendy was very respectful of what space she had. She curled the last of her hair, liking the soft waves around her face and knowing that they were going to be gone as soon as she jostled her head. "Do you have any hair spray?" It was always a tossup between hair that went limp and frizzy immediately and having crunchy hair that didn't move in a breeze. Tonight, she was up for the crunch. She had even put on makeup.

"It's in with the art supplies!" Wendy called from the sewing room. "The box marked graphite!"

"Art supplies?"

"I use it as a drawing fixative!"

Of course she did.

Addison unplugged the curling iron and, when she could find no place to put it to cool, walked around with it in one hand to find the box labeled graphite and wrestle the hair spray out of it until Wendy came out and realized what she was trying to do. "Oh here, Addy, let me get that for you. This can cool on the kitchen counter. Don't you look gorgeous! Not a date, huh?"

Addison walked very carefully back to the bathroom, hoping to keep her hard-won curls from going limp too fast. She grinned at Wendy. "Not a *real* date."

"Well, you're going to wow him like it *was* a real date," Wendy said approvingly. "Is that what you're wearing?"

Addison had showered when she finished at the day care and changed into clean jeans and a t-shirt that said 'Donut Worry, Be Happy.'

"What's wrong with this?" Was the bakery name too terrible a pun?

"It's got no cleavage!"

"I'm going out to dinner with a toddler!" Addison protested. "I don't need *cleavage!*"

"The toddler will probably appreciate the cleavage as much as Roderick does," Wendy scoffed. "They still think those things are made of milk. Hold on, I've got a shirt that you will *rock.*"

Addison knew better than to argue with Wendy, even if she could have made the point that Gabby must have been bottle fed, and she very, very carefully took the t-shirt off without disturbing her curls too completely. The shirt she got in return buttoned up the front, which at least didn't risk her coif.

"I think this is too *much* cleavage," she said, examining her reflection. "Shouldn't there be another button here?"

Wendy grinned. "Doesn't have one, sorry," she trilled. "Oh, look at the time, you'll be late if you take the time to change again!"

Addison looked at the clock in chagrin. Doing her hair had taken a good deal longer than she had hoped it would and she didn't want to keep Roderick waiting. She felt like she was buzzing with anticipation. It didn't matter that it wasn't a real date, or that Gabby would be in tow.

She ducked into her room to grab a sweater that she

could wear if she got self-conscious, and her purse. "I'll be back before ten, for sure," she told Wendy.

"I'm not setting a curfew," Wendy said with a shrug. "I won't worry unless you don't check in with me before tomorrow. Say lunch?"

"I'm not staying over!" Addison protested over her shoulder as she left.

"But you could!" Wendy sang after her.

16

*R*oderick had always considered himself a punctual man. It was important to be where he said he'd be when he said it. It was part of how his little plumbing business had done so well; he was a contractor everyone could trust to run on time.

That was before Gabby.

It was uncanny how she seemed to know exactly when it would be most inconvenient to blow out a diaper, or knock something over that needed cleaned up right away, or pitch the kind of fit that required a lengthy calm-down period.

It was the first of these that made him late to the restaurant; a diaper so brutal it required a half-body sponge bath, to Gabby's giggling delight. "Yuck!" she said as she was being wiped down. "Yuck!"

"Well, I certainly hope that's out of your system," he told her, folding the tabs of the clean diaper around her with an extra tickle. He texted Addison to let her know they were running late.

No worries, she replied with a smiley face.

She was waiting at a booth with a high chair already waiting. Gabby took one look at the tantalizing silverware and the various condiments on the table and apparently realized that the high chair would keep her from all of them. Getting her into it was like trying to stuff a cat into a carrier before a trip to the vet, all impossible bendiness and outstretched limbs, complete with yowling.

It took distracting her with a stuffy to get her strapped in at last and she banged on her tray in protest until a waitress in a cowgirl dress brought a few pages to color and a box with four cheap crayons.

Then, at last, Roderick could slip into the booth across from Addison and drink her in. "You look amazing."

Addison's hand fluttered towards the expanse of bosom that her frilly blue blouse was exposing as if it embarrassed her and turned pink. Her hair was different, the curls looser around her face, and Roderick thought that she might be wearing makeup.

He'd felt that dressing up too much was probably inappropriate, but he'd worn a nicer-than-usual collared shirt and a bolo tie, and her appreciative look made it worth the effort.

"Sorry I'm late," he added.

"Oh, it's fine," Addison promised. "No worries. I know how it is, trying to get out of the house with little ones."

"You said you were a nanny," Roderick remembered. "How old were your kids?"

"Eighteen months and five, when I started, so only a little older than Gabby. I was with the family until they were both in school, almost five years. It's crazy how fast they grow." Addison talked about them for a while, and Roderick tried not to stare down her shirt. He forgot that they were there for dinner until the waitress came to take their order and he realized that he hadn't even looked at the menu yet.

Addison ordered a barbecue chicken wrap and a soda and

Roderick hastily picked one of their country burgers, following suit with a soft drink rather than a beer, and got an order of chicken fingers for Gabby. "Rare!" he added, handing back the menus. "The burger, not the chicken fingers."

"No one wants rare chicken fingers," Addison giggled.

"Seasoned with salmonella!" Roderick joked weakly.

The waitress pretended they were funny to earn her tip and splashed water into their glasses. Gabby threw one of the crayons after her and Roderick went to pick it up. "We're not doing that right now, sweetie. Do you want to color?"

She wasn't quite to the point of scribbling with crayons, something that the developmental sites that Roderick followed assured him was just fine, like her stubborn refusal to walk. But she liked to pick them up in her fingers and crumple the coloring pages.

Most of the conversation centered around Gabby because Roderick's life did, but they talked a little about his business and Addison told him about her early care classes. "They don't want klutzes handling actual babies, of course, and one of our teachers decided that eggs weren't really challenging enough, so she sent us home with those personal-sized watermelons. Except that the watermelon she gave one of my classmates got eaten by her roommate, and when she came back to class, she was wearing a baby carrier with this behemoth thirty-pound watermelon. And she was cool as a cucumber, talking about growth spurts and weight mile-stones, even though it was totally obvious that it wasn't the same watermelon at all."

Roderick gave an embarrassing guffaw of laughter and asked, "Did she pass?"

"Flying colors," Addison promised. "I got docked points because one of the scarves I used got wet and it turned out the dye wasn't colorfast, so my precious watermelon-child had all these purple blotches on it."

"That seems unfair," Roderick protested.

"Well, I learned not to use hand-dyed things on kids. Haven't dyed a single one of them since then!"

They talked as easily in person as they had on the phone, laughing about the same things, including Gabby effortlessly in their banter. She added her own strong opinions, and when Roderick gave her a sippy cup of water, waved it around like a drunk with a tankard.

The meal was decidedly mediocre, but Roderick enjoyed it more than any meal he'd ever eaten, watching Addison's animated face as they chatted, Gabby beside him devouring chicken tenders like a small velociraptor.

"Dessert?" the bored waitress finally wanted to know.

"I couldn't," Addison groaned. "I am stuffed."

Roderick shook his head.

Gabby had slowed down and was playing with the last of her chicken. Her eyes were starting to glaze, and her fingers were getting clumsy. Clumsier.

On cue, she raised a fist and rubbed her eyes. "Oh, there it is," Addison said knowingly.

"The sleepy rub," Roderick agreed. "Think she'll stay awake all the way home?"

"I would not gamble a thin dime against it."

They got the bill, and there was a moment where they both reached for it and their hands brushed. Her touch was electric, and it was one of those slow-motion moments in a movie with swelling music.

"My treat," Roderick said firmly, not moving his hand.

"I'll get it next time," Addison conceded, and she took her hand back shyly.

Roderick belatedly remembered that her terrible previous

boyfriend had always insisted on paying, as a method of control. "I'll let you," he promised.

"Ababa," Gabby said tiredly.

Roderick left cash, with a generous tip because of the mess Gabby made, and gathered up all of her things.

"That's a bold diaper bag," Addison said approvingly when he slung the fuzzy cookie monster over his shoulder.

"Never underestimate the power of a fuzzy blue monster to act as a necessary distraction when you're trying to get kicking legs in pants," Roderick said, unbuckling Gabby. "It's worked well for me."

They walked together to the door, Gabby in Roderick's arms, and he was keenly aware of how he and Addison were looking at each other and glancing away just as quickly, both of them smiling.

Addison walked with him to his truck and he strapped Gabby in. She was barely awake enough to protest, and she made some muddy signs with her hands that might have been more or berries or gorilla.

"I hope she doesn't take a power nap on the way home and then wake up prepared to keep you up all night," Addison said wryly. "Good night, Gabby."

Gabby's head was already lolling.

Roderick shut the door on her as quietly as he could. "She's usually a good sleeper," he said, "whether she's napped or not."

It had gotten dark while they were in the restaurant, only a hint of color left in the sky, and the street lights were on. Across the lot, a group of rowdy teenagers was gathered around a car shouting good-natured insults at each other.

"I had a good time," Addison said, wrapping her sweater around herself against the evening chill.

"Even with a fourteen-month-old chaperone?" Roderick teased.

"Especially with a fourteen-month-old chaperone," Addison giggled.

Now, now, now, instinct whispered at him.

Or least, he *thought* it was instinct. It was hard to separate wanting her from wanting to be with her, from his bone-deep certainty that they could be happy together, from his wolf panting in joy because everything was simply right in the world at this very moment.

She was gazing up at him, her lips just slightly parted, her whole posture invitation and excitement. He could kiss her now, he could wrap her up in his arms and taste her at last.

"Addison..." he started, because even instinct wasn't consent.

"Yes!" she said. Then, abashed, "I mean, yes?"

They met halfway between, the barest brush of lips to lips at first, then her soft arms were up around his neck and he was trying not to crush her against him and failing more than succeeding. "Addison..." he murmured, or tried to, but there was no space for words between them.

They didn't stop kissing until the teenagers across the lot started clapping and whistling, then hastily backed apart. Addison gave an embarrassed curtsy in their direction and Roderick tipped what would have been an invisible hat as they hooted their approval.

"Another time, another place?" Addison suggested quietly.

Every time, every place, Roderick thought longingly. But he could be patient. He was more sure now than ever that Addison was meant to be with him, and he could wait for forever.

17

Addison reluctantly took her leave of Roderick, waving in chagrin to their audience, and skipped light-footedly back to her car full of moving boxes.

Of all the things she had expected to find in Nickel City, she had never seen Roderick coming.

She turned around and waved back at him when she got to her car, then slid into the driver seat and tipped her head forward to lean on the steering wheel.

She had always longed for...something of her own. A house. A family. Maybe a kid or two. She was terribly fond of all of her charges, but she always knew that they weren't wholly hers. And with Owen, she hadn't even felt like her own *self*.

Now, it felt like she had a chance. A chance at someone who looked at her like Roderick looked at her. A chance to be Gabby's real mother. A chance to be kissed like Roderick kissed her.

Her skin tingled with longing and excitement.

Instinct? Magic? A *mate?*

It was like she was in a fairy tale.

After a moment, she reminded herself that the teenagers were probably still watching her and Roderick had long since driven away to put Gabby to bed. She pulled out of the lot and drove back to Wendy's tiny house.

"How'd the shirt work out?" Wendy wanted to know. The mannequin in the living room had been abandoned and Wendy was knitting something in front of a sitcom. "Twelve, thirteen, hang on, I dropped a stitch, crap, here you are, fourteen, fifteen, sixteen, purl. I should know better than to try to do this and watch *Letterkenny* at the same time." She put the knitting aside and made room on the couch for Addison, tossing aside an afghan, her yarn bag, and two of the ugliest throw pillows Addison had ever seen. "I need all the dirt," she commanded. "Did you kiss him?"

Addison flopped onto the couch. "The shirt worked *great,*" she said honestly.

"I bet he couldn't keep his eyes off you for a second," Wendy said with great satisfaction. "How was the chaperone?"

"A good conversation piece," Addison giggled.

"And the kiss?" Wendy demanded.

The *kiss.*

Addison had certainly never been kissed like that before and she felt like her face would split from smiling. Her lips felt *used.*

Wendy made a noise like a steam kettle ready to boil. "Tell me about the kiss!"

"He has great lips," Addison decided she could safely say. Great lips, and a great mouth, and a great tongue, and a great, hard body that she could have pressed herself against all day.

"Great lips," Wendy said in disbelief. "That's what you put in a Yelp review. Did you get to second base?"

"You don't get to bases on a guy," Addison protested. "Man nipple just isn't the same."

"Fine," Wendy scoffed. "Then, did you let *him* get to second base?"

Addison shook her head a little regretfully, remembering how his hands had felt at her waist, not wanting them to move from there, ever, and at the same time desperate for him to touch more.

"Did you get a second date at least?" Wendy asked, exasperated. "C'mon, Addison, I have no life and I have to live vicariously through you. Throw me a bone!"

"This *was* our second date," Addison pointed out. She used her opposite foot to pry each shoe off and tucked her stockinged feet up underneath her. "We had lunch two days ago."

"Good lord," Wendy said in frustration. "It's going to take you a month to get laid at this rate."

Addison hid her face in the ugliest of the throw pillows. "Wend-y!"

"Just because I live like a nun, doesn't mean everyone needs to," Wendy pointed out. "Now, as much as I love having you here, we have got to get you your own place, with a much better bed, because that will probably help a lot. Air mattresses squeak."

Addison gave a groan. "Everything costs soooooo much," she complained. "I haven't saved anything yet for the deposits that they want, and I'm worried that if Veronica raises the rent on Cherry's place, I won't even have a *job*." She looked at Wendy over the pillow. "I hate to impose. I really hoped I'd find a place in a week or two, but that's looking stunningly unlikely."

"Oh, yeah, about that!" Wendy bounced up and went to a pile of mail. "There's a municipality meeting in a few weeks. They're trying to pass some restrictions on the short-term rentals and put a freeze on rent hikes. Believe me, you are not the only one having this problem right now."

She handed Addison a flyer.

Addison took it and skimmed the information. "A town meeting? They still have those?"

"It's an assembly meeting with public testimony. You should give some."

"I've been here less than a week," Addison chuckled. "I have nowhere to live. I'm pretty sure I don't count as their voting public."

"Get your boyfriend to testify," Wendy suggested with an eyebrow waggle. "He lives here and probably wants to keep his neighborhoods for neighbors."

"Catchy slogan."

"Neighborhoods for neighbors? Oh, you should paint signs and have your day care kids march around downtown holding them. You can't lose!"

"I am not exploiting a bunch of children for cheap rent," Addison scoffed.

"Why don't you move in with Roderick?" Wendy said, laughing, but the joke fell short and Addison went cold.

She'd moved in with Owen for reasons of convenience, and just look how that had worked out. She wasn't going to make that same mistake again. Not based on something as uncertain and fickle as instinct.

Wendy wasn't oblivious to Addison's reaction. "Sorry, too soon?"

"Too soon is the story of my life," Addison said. "Last time—"

"Roderick isn't Owen," Wendy said unnecessarily.

"Not even close," Addison said with a little hitch to her breath. She didn't even need instinct to tell her that, though it was a humming undertone to her certainty. "It's just..."

"Once bitten, twice shy?" Wendy guessed, once Addison had trailed off.

"Once bitten, twice *smart*," Addison corrected.

18

*R*oderick knew he was a lucky dad. He'd rubbed elbows with enough other parents to hear the horror stories about kids Gabby's age that refused to sleep. But most nights, Gabby went to bed with minimal fuss—a few moments of crying at most—and woke up full of bubbles and joy.

So he was surprised when Gabby woke him screaming at just past midnight, about a week after his first date with Addison.

Bleary-eyed, he staggered down the hall to her bedroom and opened the door. "What's wrong, sweetheart? What's the problem?"

Her diaper was dry and she refused food when he offered it. Picking her up didn't calm her, singing didn't work. He tried to settle her with a book, but she arched her back and fought him, kicking at the book and crying. He tried music, television, different food, changing her diaper even though it wasn't wet. "What do you need, Gabby? What's wrong?"

She signed for milk, then pushed it away, weeping in frustration, and by about three AM, Roderick was tempted to join her in pitching a fit. "I want to help you, baby girl, I want to help you, but I don't know what you want, darling girl."

At last Gabby seemed to run out of steam, and although she didn't seem interested in sleeping, she was content to sob against Roderick's shoulder while he paced the house.

"Poor baby," he told her, over and over again, and he tried to put her down in the crib twice before giving that up in the face of her distress.

Then he finally felt it, a little tickle in his tired head that made his wolf whine in understanding.

"Oh, honey, are you ready for this?" Roderick wasn't sure if what he felt was relief or fear. "Am I?"

Gabby was going to be a shifter.

Not today, probably, maybe not for days or even months, but she was starting the process. It was like teething, supposedly, but even worse, to hear Ian's stories. Gabby already had six teeth that had been days worth of agony apiece, but Roderick knew that it would feel like a walk in the park compared to what was coming next.

Would she be a wolf, like him? Or a domestic cat like his maternal grandmother? A throwback to something further back in his lines? Dana wasn't a shifter, and she had been gone, at least emotionally, before Roderick had a chance to talk about it. When it was clear that she wasn't going to be a part of Gabby's life, Roderick had seen no reason to bring up the topic with her. If she had shifter ancestors, he wasn't sure how to ask, and he didn't have a way to contact her now, anyway.

Gabby went limp on his shoulder, and he paced with her a little longer, not willing to risk disturbing her by putting her down. At least he had an answer now, that was some comfort.

When his shoulder was damp with her drool and she was

snoring gently, he was finally able to lay her down in the crib and creep away.

* * *

The morning was exactly as awful as he guessed it would be, dry eyes opening to the shrill of his alarm.

The prospect of a date with Addison that evening was the only thing that made his breakfast bearable.

He sucked down coffee like a lifeline before daring to go in to wake Gabby, letting her sleep a little extra to make up for their fractured night.

She seemed no worse for their lack of sleep, though she was inclined to be fussy about food and was perhaps a touch more clingy than usual. Roderick was able to distract her without too much trouble and she sat quietly with a board book looking at her favorite pages while he texted Addison that they were going to be late, gathered up her diaper bag, checked his voicemail, and made a few calls to schedule repairs. He liked to have a free block in the morning for emergency calls that needed priority, and he smiled at the block on his calendar for the evening.

Addison.

Ian had agreed to take Gabby so that they could have an actual-factual, no-chaperone date. Roderick wished that he was facing the day with better sleep, but he was still filled with anticipation and excitement. Their single stolen kiss was like a promise, and he'd cleaned the house, just in case he brought her back here afterward.

"Ready to go, Gabby? Want to go see Cherry? And Addison?"

"Ababba addy," she replied, stretching her arms out to him. She probably wasn't saying Addy's name on purpose, Roderick told himself, but it still made his heart feel a size larger and he echoed his wolf's satisfaction as he scooped Gabby into his arms.

All the satisfaction vanished into shock and alarm when he came out of his house and found a woman waiting at his mailbox as if she was afraid to come to the door.

He recognized her from that distance, even though she was thinner than she'd been the last time he saw her, and her hair was shockingly short and in natural curls; she'd always worn it straightened, or tightly braided. Tamed, she liked to say.

There was something wilder about her now, and Roderick folded his arms around Gabby a little tighter and resisted his urge to swap sides with her to hold her a little further away.

She took one step towards him as he walked to his parked truck, then stopped and waited for him to close the distance.

"Dana," he said warily. "What are you doing here?"

He was desperately afraid that he already knew.

19

"*R*ough night," Roderick's text said. "We'll be late."

So Addison didn't worry at first when the morning went by without a sign of Gabby and Roderick. She texted him back a hasty thumbs up and chasing the kids kept her busy and distracted. When she did pause to think about them, it was with wistful longing for the evening ahead. A real date! At a restaurant without kids! And afterward…

Amy broke out in frustrated wails when the older kids refused to let her play with them, and turned into a sulky owl, screeching her displeasure. Addison scampered to distract her back to happy babbling and—most importantly—her human form.

She looked up when Tara appeared at her elbow, expecting her to want to play at some make-believe. But Tara didn't have a bandage to apply or a doll to talk to, she only gazed at Addison with her dark, solemn eyes and said, "I want to shift."

Addison gave a quick look around the room, doing a headcount of the kids. Cherry was setting up a craft and Shea was sitting with the babies. Addison stood up and Tara slipped her hand trustingly into hers.

Cherry looked up and met her gaze—she might not have shifter instinct, but she seemed to be almost supernaturally sensitive to everything that happened in her school. She nodded and called cheerfully to Amy, "Come help me count, Amy! One! Two! Three!"

Amy toddled eagerly to Cherry and Addison walked with Tara to the back door and out into the back yard. Addison sat on the grass near the middle of the lawn, letting Tara pick wherever made her comfortable to shift.

Tara didn't go for the corner of the yard that was in the bright sunlight, but for the shadow-dappled corner under one of the big, spreading maple trees and she stood still so long in human form that Addison thought she was going to change her mind.

Then she shivered in place and shifted, skillfully taking her clothing with her, and Addison finally understood.

Tara wasn't the pearl-white, golden-horned unicorn that her sticker showed, she was all mud-brown and covered in subtle rainbow-hued scales, with a fuzzy silvery-brown mane all around her neck like a lion. A short, furry crest traced her spine and ended in a tufted tail. She had small antlers on both sides of her narrow head, with one prong forward in a broad point.

Delicate cloven hooves lifted, one after another, and her big, deer-like ears flattened back against her head as it drooped sadly. Long whiskers around her muzzle floated in the air currents as if they were weightless. She looked a little like an Eastern dragon and a deer, mixed up with a Western unicorn.

"Oh, Tara," Addison said in wonder. "You aren't ugly at all." But she understood Tara's misplaced shame; she looked nothing like the books about unicorns on the day care library shelves, or the cartoons on the other children's' backpacks and t-shirts. "You *are* a unicorn, a Chinese unicorn. Do you know much about them?"

Tara's head cocked hopefully and shook a no, her undulous whiskers following her face.

"They're called *kirin*," Addison explained. "To be honest, I don't know much about them, except that they are very rare and special. You are amazing, Tara. You have nothing to be embarrassed about. You don't have to show your friends if you don't want to, but I know that they would still like you."

Tara stepped cautiously closer and finally put her head in Addison's outstretched hand with a huff of breath. Then she shifted seamlessly into her human form and crawled into Addison's lap as a little girl.

Addison wrapped her arms around Tara, leaning over to comfort her and snuggle her in close. They sat quietly like that for some time, until the back door of the day care burst open and disgorged two boys, pelting out onto the lawn.

"We're going to play Simon-Says-Shift and I'm going to remember MY CLOTHES!" Gil announced.

Tara sat up and wiped a dirty hand across her face. Addison wasn't sure if she'd actually been crying, but there were no tears in her eyes now. She glanced once at Addison for support, then stood up and brushed off her heart-covered pants. "Can I play?" she asked shyly, and Gil and Robert didn't hesitate a moment to draw her to the starting line and start explaining the rules over each other.

Addison ducked her head into the classroom to see if there were any other children who wanted to play, and to exchange an enthusiastic thumbs up with Cherry.

None of the children reacted in the slightest when Tara shifted along with the rest of them. When she won the noisy game with a final fleet-footed dash to Addison on the finish line, Gil was inclined to pout, but Robert simply pointed out,

"She shifts better than you do." None of them seemed even the slightest bit curious about what she was; she was still Tara, and she shifted better than the boys.

Addison gave her a sticker—a bear eating out of a pot of honey—and Tara proudly peeled off the backing and stuck it to her shirt.

Gil had to go back and collect his socks, though he had technically remembered the rest of his clothing, so he hadn't been disqualified from the game or sent back to the beginning.

Addison coordinated a handful of other games, cheerfully amending the rules when Amy came out to join them, toddling among them and shifting into her owl form to beat her downy wings at random points.

"It's book time!" Cherry called from the door. "Who wants to help me pick which book we read?"

"Firefighters to the Rescue!" Robert cried.

"Corduroy!" Tara shouted.

"Pigeon!" Gil shouted louder.

"Aaaaaah!" Amy added, falling over on her face when she tried to run too fast.

Addison helped her back up, picked up Gil's shoes again, and herded them all back inside, exchanging a grin with Cherry.

Three books later, after Addison and Shea had fed the babies and helped get everyone down for quiet time on their nap mats, she sat down in one of the undersized chairs at the far side of the room with a scrap of paper and a crayon and wrote down some ideas that occurred to her before she could forget them.

She was folding up the note to fit in her pocket when Cherry came to sit across the table from her.

"Did everything work out okay?" she asked quietly.

"It's all fine," Addison promised. "Tara is a kirin."

When Cherry looked at her blankly, she explained, "A Chinese unicorn. They look like a dragon and deer hybrid. Is there a library in town? I thought I might see if I could check out some books so she could see herself in print."

"Next block over, behind the bakery," Cherry said. "Her mother only ever said unicorn, and I never thought to ask! I had no idea!" She shook her head. "Here I was, showing her all the books with Western unicorns and pointing out Amy's shirt. Addison, I feel like a *clod*."

"You didn't know," Addison said kindly. "And I'm sure she'll face that a lot, I mean I didn't even realize they were *real*."

"We can do better," Cherry said firmly, then louder, "Gil, we're pretending to be still like statues! Statues don't wiggle!"

There were some giggles from the nap mats. One of the babies in the nursery corner began to fuss and Addison got to her feet to go check on her. When she returned, Cherry asked, "What do you think of the name The Little Zoo for the day care?"

Addison considered, looking around at the cages of animals. "It would work," she said. "It does imply a certain amount of chaos."

"And maybe too much truth in advertising," Cherry chuckled. "I want to imply shifting, without coming right out and saying it. I'll keep thinking." She frowned briefly, looking for a moment very vulnerable and lost.

"Are you worried about Veronica raising the rent?" Addison guessed.

Cherry gave a bright smile that couldn't fool Addison. "We'll figure something out," she promised, but Addison could tell that behind her cheer she was quite concerned.

Addison glanced at the clock. Gabby and Roderick still hadn't shown up, and she wondered if she should be worried.

She shook her head firmly. All she knew about Roderick, she'd learned in a few not-really-dates and a couple of toddler hand-offs, plus the notes on his guardian-contact sheet and a handful of long, rambling telephone conversations and so many texts that she'd had to change her phone plan. It felt like she knew him, but what did she really know?

Maybe he tended to run late a lot. Maybe something had come up, and he didn't feel a need to send a second message. Lots of things might have happened.

Even if what they had *was* instinct, there was a limit to what they owed each other.

20

"I know what the papers say," Dana said defensively. "I know. I just...things came up, and I thought we could talk."

Roderick tried to resolve the woman before her with the whirlwind emotional upheaval that she had been in his heart before. The months before Gabby's birth had been a rollercoaster of simultaneously wanting to work out a relationship with Dana and being grateful that she wanted nothing to do with him long-term, trying to make sense of his instinct, or the sudden lack of direction from it. He had expected their next meeting to have the same kind of internal conflict and he was shocked that he didn't have any lingering feelings over the mother of his child.

When he looked at Dana, he measured her against Addison, a woman he'd only known a week, and didn't want her at all.

Instinct knows, his wolf said smugly.

"Why are you here?" he asked Dana. "Why *now?*" Gabby was starting to fuss, the tingly not-quite-shifter feel of her intensifying briefly. He bounced her gently, and she settled. It should take at least a few days before she was a true shifting risk, Roderick thought, but it would be just his kind of luck if she turned into a wolf cub *right now.* He was really hoping that she was going to give him a few weeks or months. Baby-proofing and wolf-proofing were similar, but not exactly the same, and he wasn't sure where house training fit with any of the rest of her milestones. The baby books were completely unhelpful on that topic.

"Can we go somewhere?" Dana asked plaintively. "Just to talk." She glanced back at the house but didn't suggest it.

"We're heading to the day care," Roderick said, not caring that he didn't sound particularly accommodating. "And I have jobs to get to."

"Later, then," Dana said quickly. "I can come back." But to Roderick's horror, there were tears welling up in her eyes.

Whatever ill will Roderick might hold crumbled in the face of her misery. "I already told the day care I was going to be late. Come on in and have a cup of coffee. Gabby needs a new diaper already, anyway."

Was he being a doormat? Gabby was staring at Dana with round stranger-eyes, doubtful and cautious. And why shouldn't she? Dana *was* a stranger to her. A stranger who just happened to be her mother.

He unlocked the house and stepped aside as she came in.

"It looks good," she said faintly, as he took Gabby back to her changing pad and efficiently took care of the gift she'd produced for him. "You look good."

Roderick gave her a suspicious, sideways look. Was she expecting to pick things up where they'd left off? Did she think that he'd spent the last year pining over her?

Her next words dispelled that worry. "I'm not here to get back together, or try to take Gabriella away from you."

"Then what do you want?" Roderick asked, not letting any warmth into his voice. He didn't particularly feel any warmth. He didn't bear this woman any ill will, but he didn't owe her anything, either, and her sudden return put worry in the pit of his stomach. Was she going to be trouble? Would she ruin what he was building with Addison? Even if he didn't think that Dana would deliberately try to sabotage Roderick's new relationship, having an ex around felt like a complication he didn't need or want.

They went into the kitchen and he turned on the coffee pot. He'd bought one of the coffee makers that used pods; he didn't like how much packaging he threw out, but he liked his second cup being as fresh as the first one. He put Gabby into her high chair and gave her a handful of crackers, then set a cup under the dispenser, waiting for the water to heat up.

"Boobuh!" Gabby said in disdain. She looked at her hands in frustration, put her fingers together, and twisted her wrists. It was as close as she had come to mastering the sign for blueberry.

Normally, he might insist that she at least try the food in front of her, but Roderick was desperate to forestall a fuss so that he could try to figure out exactly what was going on. He went to the fridge and got a few blueberries to put on her tray. She gave a cry of triumph and fell upon them. Roderick caught Dana staring.

"She's...so big," she said when she looked up and saw Roderick watching her. "I didn't expect... I don't know what I expected."

"I'm really hoping we can get to a point soon," Roderick said wryly. "Those aren't going to distract her for long, and I've got a job later this morning."

Dana licked her lips. "I can't have any more kids."

That certainly was a point.

It hit Roderick like a fist in the gut. First, he was sorry for Dana, for the terrible finality in her voice and the unexpected pain on her face. Fear followed on the tail of that sympathy. Did she want to stake some kind of claim on Gabby? Did she think that the two of them could pick up where they'd left off, like he hadn't moved on? Their time together had been fun, but they'd never had a relationship worth a name, and he couldn't imagine making a home with her. Should he ask *why* she couldn't have children? Wait for her to volunteer more information? His mind swirled with possible dangers in this minefield of a conversation.

"I'm sorry to hear that," he finally said, circling back to his first reaction. "Is there something I can do?"

To his horror, Dana began to cry. "I don't know," she sobbed. "I shouldn't have come. I can't take Gabby away, and I don't want to get back together, I don't think. I just...I had to come and see her. I wanted to know that I'd done one thing in my life right, to see her again, to know that she was...okay."

Roderick wanted to comfort her, but feared it would encourage something he didn't want to. *What do I do?* he asked his wolf, but his wolf had no advice. Where was instinct when he needed the damn thing?

He settled for making a cup of coffee while Dana found the paper towels hanging by the sink and loudly blew her nose.

When she had returned to her seat, the coffee finished brewing, and he put the cup in front of her. "There's sugar," he offered gruffly.

"No, thank you," she said quietly. She took a sip and cradled her fingers around the mug like she could use the heat to give her strength.

Gabby, having run out of blueberries, babbled into the silence commandingly. "Boobuh! Boobuh!" She smashed a berry-stained cracker.

"We're doing good," Roderick said. He brought the container of blueberries out of the fridge and tipped a generous helping out onto her tray.

Gabby stared at the bounty and then, almost grudgingly, offered him one. He took it. "Thanks, honey."

"Addy," she said in reply, then she was entertaining herself chasing the berries around her tray and putting them mostly in her mouth.

Roderick got his own cup of coffee and wondered if he'd regret the extra on top of a night that was low on sleep. He sat across from Dana, who was watching Gabby with a mixture of hunger and regret.

"Should we have a lawyer here?" he asked.

It must have come out more warningly than he intended.

Dana gave him a stricken look, then shook her head. "No. No, it's not like that. I'll go whenever you ask me to."

"You...don't want visitation rights or something?"

Dana wilted. "I don't know what I want. I thought I did, before. I was so sure. But this has...hit me a lot harder than I expected it to." She lifted her chin. "I've always been honest with you, Roderick. We didn't see eye to eye on a lot of things, but I never led you on, and I never lied. And I'm not lying about this. I honestly don't know what to do from here. My...my boyfriend left me when he found out, and it broke my heart. It scared me that...maybe I'd done that to you. I knew you'd take good care of Gabby, but I worried that I'd done you wrong and I don't like to leave debts."

Had she broken his heart? Roderick remembered how gutted he'd been, and how adrift those first few months had been...and how Gabby had been the glue that held him together. He looked at Dana, at the proud line of her neck and the set of her jaw. He'd felt betrayed, and he'd been angry at times, but he hadn't been broken, because he hadn't ever seen them with a future together...even when he'd desperately wanted one. Instinct had told him that they were meant to be together, then gone coldly, oddly silent when Dana chose a different path.

She'd tested his pride, but she hadn't touched his heart. Not the way Addison had in the short time they'd known each other.

Was it just instinct, the way he couldn't look at Addison without feeling like his feet were finally on the right path? He'd tried to force Dana to his vision of their destiny, and it had been the wrong future for both of them. Instinct was showed you a chance, his mother had told him.

Dana's face fell as she took his silence for rejection. "I'm sorry for everything that's happened, but I'm not sorry I came," she said quietly. "It looks like you've got everything under control and I'm really happy for both of you. It's enough to know that."

Roderick suspected that if he told Dana to go, she would go and that would be the end of it. He and Gabby would never see her again.

He looked at Gabby, who had dropped a blueberry in her lap but not noticed its escape and could not figure out why it was no longer in her hand.

And if Dana stayed, she would ask no more of them than he was absolutely willing to give.

His instinct, when he unfolded it from all the emotion swirling inside him, told him that she would do as she promised, whichever he chose. He was the one holding the cards.

"I'm not sorry you came, either," Roderick said gently. "And I can't be sorry for everything that happened, because if it hadn't, I wouldn't have Gabby." He wouldn't have been happy without Gabby, he realized, and instinct knew that.

Hearing her name, Gabby waved a fist. "Addy!" she said.

And without Gabby, he wouldn't have Addison, either.

"I've got a few things to catch you up on," he told Dana. "But first, let me introduce you to your daughter."

21

ddison knew that something was wrong the moment Roderick walked into the day care.

No...not wrong. She tried to sort her instinct from her observations, and it did nothing but hum unhelpfully. There was something a little different about Roderick; his usual easy smile was missing. He looked distant and concerned.

"What's up?" she asked quietly, as she took Gabby over the gate so that Roderick wouldn't have to take off his boots.

"Addy!" Gabby sang. "Boobuh abada!"

Addison was grateful that Gabby had warmed up to her so quickly. Having her wail when Roderick left the first few days had been hard on everyone involved.

"Dana's in town. She came to see me."

It took Addison a moment to place the name. "Gabby's mom," she said, and it made a tangle of confusing feelings in her chest. Jealousy, worry, fear. She wanted to protect Roderick and fight for this new thing that they had, and she was terrified that maybe...she shouldn't. Roderick wasn't hers, not really. Maybe it would be better if he and Gabby's mother were together. Better for Gabby, better for Roderick.

Roderick frowned. "We're not getting back together," he said firmly. "You don't have to worry about that."

Addison wondered if she was that transparent. "Still," she offered gently, "this has to...complicate things."

Did they still have a date for that night? Was Dana here for long? Did she want to place some claim on Gabby? Questions that Addison didn't dare ask crowded into her brain.

What did this mean? Addison tried to focus on her shifter senses. She could feel that Roderick was tense, that Gabby was happy, that the other children were safe...but the magic gave her no clues, no draw towards the best thing to do. It also gave her no twang of warning, which she hoped was a good sign.

"I don't want it to," Roderick said, still frowning.

It took Addison a moment to backtrack through her thoughts and realized that *complication* was what he didn't want.

"You have to think about what's best for you," Addison said slowly. "And best for Gabby." Even if that wasn't *her*.

Roderick sucked in his breath and Addison thought that if the gate weren't between them, he might have reached for her. Cherry called a cheerful greeting from across the room just then and Gabby bounced in Addison's arms. She didn't seem at all bothered by the appearance of her mother and Addison envied her that innocence.

Then she abruptly recognized the nuances of what her instinct *was* telling her. "Gabby's...?"

"A shifter," Roderick finished. "Or will be, soon."

"You *have* had an exciting morning," Addison said sympathetically. Then, hesitantly, "Is...?" It would be nice if she could figure out how to finish her own questions.

"Dana's not a shifter," Roderick said, somehow knowing exactly what she was wondering. "We never got to the point where I told her about shifters, either."

Gabby was getting impatient and wanted down, so Addison set her down on her feet. Gabby held onto her knees for a few moments, looked like she was considering steps, then fell to all fours and crawled towards Cherry and the other kids.

"So *extra* complicated," Addison said, shaking her head. "With sprinkles of problematic." Did she even have the right to ask what he planned to do next? "Do you want to put off our date?"

When he didn't answer right away, Addison hastily added, "It's okay if you do. I totally understand. I know we aren't, we haven't, I mean...it's not like..."

She had unconsciously stepped back from the gate and Roderick looked like he wanted to step over it. "I'd still like to go out," he said. "This doesn't change anything between us."

Didn't it?

He'd said that he and Dana were never really a thing, but there had still been feelings—complicated feelings—and they'd had a *child* together. No one came through something like that without a little baggage.

Addison thought that he was sincere, that he still wanted her, the way that she still wanted him, but instinct didn't have a great sense of nuance, and she sometimes doubted that it understood mundane things like paying bills and car insurance...or negotiating custody. It had been a terrible conflict in her soul, not knowing *how* to leave Owen when she finally understood that every fiber of her being told her she ought to.

But Roderick wasn't Owen, she kept having to remind herself, and she wasn't the same naive girl that Owen had preyed upon.

"I'd still like to go out, too," Addison said, realizing that she had left him waiting long enough that he was shifting his weight from foot to foot nervously.

He looked relieved and Addison was surprised how much that soothed her own ruffled feelings. She flushed, suddenly remembering their passionate kiss. Would he have third-date expectations?

Did she want him to have them?

"I'll pick you up at six," Roderick offered. "I can show you the scenic route, point out a few of the Nickel City features."

Addison momentarily wanted to protest. Ever since Owen, she preferred to drive herself to dates, to always have an escape route, a way to get home on her own. But Roderick wasn't Owen, she remembered before she could answer. "That would be great." She trusted Roderick.

And despite the sudden return of his ex to add a whole new level of complexity to their budding relationship, Addison was definitely having third-date expectations of her own.

Gabby was not nearly as excited about her playdate with Lucy as Lucy was, especially since she could clearly tell that Roderick was going to leave her alone there in an act of cruel abandonment. She cried piteously and pulled herself up on the couch.

"We'll be fine," Ian promised, already looking a little wild around the eyes. "Take your time. It's a weekend, so we can stay up late, or if it goes really well, just drop me a text, and we'll make her up a bed."

"Baby!" Lucy declared. "She can be baby!"

When Roderick fled, Lucy was trying to put Gabby in a crib for a doll and Ian was patiently explaining that she wouldn't fit and that Lucy had to play games they both liked.

"Good luck!" he called back to Ian.

"You, too!" he replied.

Feeling rather sorry for Ian, Roderick climbed back up into his truck and drove to Addison's cousin Wendy's house. It was a tiny house in a quiet neighborhood, the little yard cluttered with sculptures, gnomes, twirling pinwheels, and banners. There was some kind of knitted sweater around one of the trees in the front yard.

Addison must have been watching for him because Roderick had only just turned off the truck and opened the door when she came out of the house. Roderick had to pause before he stepped out because she looked like a vision.

She was wearing heels and a short dress that Roderick thought must be the little black dress that all women apparently wanted. It had a somewhat higher neckline than the blouse that had driven him so crazy on their last date, but it made up for it by caressing every curve and hugging every line of her beautiful body. She had done that thing with her hair again that made it soft, bouncy curls, and her lips were scarlet red.

Roderick remembered to get the rest of the way out of the truck and went around to meet her at the passenger door. He hesitated before he opened it, in order to drink her in. "You look...amazing," he said honestly.

She flushed but seemed to be looking at him with just as much admiration. "Thank you," she said shyly. "You, too."

Roderick had decided a casual suit wasn't inappropriate for the occasion, and he was glad of that, now, because she looked like she was ready to step into the pages of a magazine and he didn't want her to think he wasn't taking this every bit as seriously.

Because he was definitely taking this seriously.

This was the woman he had been working towards his entire life. Every decision had led to her, every choice, every whisper of his wolf that he'd listened to.

She smiled but squirmed under his regard and Roderick realized that he still hadn't opened the door for her. "Let me get that," he said quickly.

It was a tall truck, and Addison looked up at it in consternation. "Goodness, I hope I don't split my skirt getting up there. Why did I think heels were smart?"

Without thinking, Roderick said, "Here, I'll help you," and it was the perfect excuse to put his hands at her waist and lift her up into the truck.

She gave a squeak of delighted surprise and got her foot into the footwell and her hand on the grab handle. She smiled down at him. "That was fun," she giggled.

Fun didn't start to cover it; the feeling of her body in his hands was like delicious torture and Roderick didn't want to let go in the slightest.

He did anyway, waited for her to swing into her seat, and shut the door, glad that it latched on the first try so he didn't have to embarrass himself by having to slam it on her a second time.

"Where are you taking me?" Addison asked when he slid into the driver's seat. She was buckled in, with the straps making interesting accents to her skimpy dress.

"Larry's," Roderick said. "Best steaks in Montana, which is saying a lot, and they usually have a decent band if you want to do any dancing."

"Oh, gosh, I really *shouldn't* have worn the heels," Addison said, but she sounded delighted. "I haven't been out dancing since college."

Roderick drove her around the town the long way, pointing out some of the major sights. He took her to the overlook of Belle Lake and she hissed in her breath at the view. "I knew Montana was beautiful," she said in awe, "but this is...amazing."

The lake was a still mirror of mountains and forests, in more colors than mountains and forests ought to be. The sky above was just starting to fade from its mid-day blue, and a few picturesque clouds looked like a painter had carefully placed them in the sky. They watched it change hues until Roderick was afraid they'd lose their reservation.

Larry's was a better-looking establishment than the name implied, and they were met at the curb by a starch-suited man who valet-parked his truck without comment. The hostess checked their name in the log and led them to a private table by a water feature.

Addison held onto his arm as they walked and was lighter on her feet than her reservations about her heels implied she would be. "This is so nice," she said, as a waiter held her chair and spread a napkin in her lap.

Roderick took his own seat and napkin and gazed at her across the table as she ran her fingers over the fancy silverware and picked up her menu.

"Addison…"

She put down the menu and smiled at him.

He didn't want to ruin the moment, but, even more, he didn't want to leave stumbling blocks between them to catch them by surprise later, either. "About Dana…"

Her smile faltered but didn't completely fade. "You don't have to explain anything," she said. "I know that this must be a lot to work out."

Roderick took a breath and let it out carefully. "I don't want Dana back. I don't think I ever had Dana. I want you, Addison. I want us. Instinct tells me that you are for me in a way that I never imagined. You are my happiness, you are my destiny."

Her face went through a dozen different expressions, all of them fascinating to watch: astonishment, longing, wariness, confusion, desire…some that Roderick couldn't even identify.

"I feel that way, too," she said at last, so quietly that Roderick had to strain to hear her over the fountain. "But we don't have to rush right into it. Sort out what you have to do with Dana. I know you have to figure out what's best for Gabby first, and I'm...I'm not going to go anywhere while you do."

That tingling magic that was a little like recognizing another shifter was back, but like a whole swarm of bees in his chest, all of them together making a happy chorus of joy.

She was more than he deserved, so gorgeous and sensible and full of kindness.

"If roles were reversed, I am not sure I would be so reasonable," Roderick confessed. "I'd want to hit him in the mouth for hurting for you."

"I'd let you," Addison chuckled wryly. "But my ex was a controlling ass that I barely escaped from. From what you've said, Dana was just scared and confused and clearly didn't know what she was letting go of. It's her loss, frankly."

"I didn't really want to make our dinner about our exes," Roderick said sheepishly.

"Then let's not," Addison suggested, picking up her menu. "I'll remind you that this one is my treat."

Roderick had forgotten that promise. "I didn't mean to make you take the more expensive meal," he said with chagrin. "I wish I'd taken you somewhere...ah..."

"Cheaper?"

"Less extravagant," Roderick conceded. "I feel like I tricked you into something."

Addison smiled slowly then, and it was full of warmth. "I hope we'll have many chances in the future to make it even."

They talked about the menu choices, then, and ordered drinks, and didn't mention exes again that night.

23

Addison's feet ached by the end of the night. Roderick persuaded her to dance for a few songs, but she thought that even just walking from the parking lot and back would have left her complaining about her shoes. They were terribly impractical and she could not wait to kick them off.

They talked over their meal, and while they were dancing, and it was just as easy in person as it had been with their very first phone call. Every story was new, every revelation was interesting. He liked very different music than she did, but they geeked out over the same television and movies. They compared reading habits and found that they had, perhaps not surprisingly, read a great number of the same baby books.

"Every one of my teachers hated the *What To Expect* books," Addison told him. "Genuine way to raise neurosis in any parent."

"They may as well have called them Fear-mongering for Fathers," Roderick agreed. "I own the one- and two-year-old books."

"Did you know they made a movie out of the first book?"

"How would you make a movie out of that book?"

"I never saw it, but I assume it was a horror movie," Addison said.

Roderick dropped his voice. "The call is coming from...the baby monitor!"

His phone gave a squawk then, and they both jumped a little and then giggled. It was a series of photographs from his babysitter: Gabby playing with a little girl several months older than she was. Gabby with food smeared across her face. Gabby with big eyes and a baby squirrel on her head.

They laughed until the waiter checked on them in concern.

"I've had so much fun," Addison told Roderick as she gathered up her purse and wondered if she would regret the second mojito she had ordered. Roderick had stopped at one beer, as the driver, but she had just enough to drink to feel slightly floaty. It was just too bad for her feet that it hadn't actually made her lighter.

She paid their bill, and they went outside to wait for the valet while the sky turned violet overhead. She shivered and Roderick wrapped his arms around her. He was so warm, so solid, so...he turned a little just as she recognized the specific pressure he was exerting against her accidentally and was suddenly, keenly aware of the tension between them.

She felt like her whole body was sizzling, and all she had to do was turn in his arms and he would take her, right there in the restaurant parking lot, they were both so on fire for each other. It was hard to say what was instinct, what was just attraction, and what was a warm friendship that was already blooming into trust. She'd come in his truck, to a place she didn't know, without a backup plan better than 'call Wendy.'

And it felt perfectly right.

The truck pulled up in front of them and the valet hurried around to open the door for her. Roderick lifted her up into the seat again, but let his hands linger just a moment. It was easy to lean over and he looked up at the right moment to catch her kiss.

His hand on her thigh tightened, but they kept the kiss light and teasing, a promise of more to come.

Roderick's phone gave an alarm then, and he glanced at it and then shared the photograph with her: Gabby asleep in a toddler bed with a squirrel in her arms like a stuffed animal.

"See you tomorrow morning," the text with it read. "I have plenty of blueberries for breakfast."

Addison licked her lips, wondering if the implication was what she thought it was.

Roderick's voice was low and full of gravel. "Would you like to come over?"

She should have him drop her back at Wendy's, Addison thought. That would be the sensible choice. The taking-it-slow choice. She surprised herself by saying, softly, "I'd like that."

Roderick's face lit up; he hadn't entirely been expecting her to say yes, and she decided that she quite liked that he wasn't making those third-date assumptions.

Their drive to his house was quieter than the trip to the restaurant, and more direct, going straight through town rather than around the hills surrounding it.

Addison wondered what he was thinking, watching his profile as he drove, occasionally catching his glances.

They were both thinking about sex, she knew. What would it be like? What would it *mean?*

Instinct felt like a neon arrow; it had never been so unmistakable.

Roderick's house was in a quiet neighborhood and it was considerably less...bachelor than Addison had envisioned that it would be. It was clearly Gabby-proof, with lower bookcase shelves full of board books and toys and higher shelves crowded with baby books next to thrillers and art references.

They were back to a place where they weren't quite sure what to do with each other, their longing warring with respect warring with their own respective histories. "I'd love to see some of your artwork," Addison remembered, eying the paintings on the walls. They were mostly landscapes; had he painted them?

Roderick got adorably flustered. "I've got some sketch-books," he said hesitantly. "Would you like a drink?"

Addison's second mojito was almost worn off, but she declined. She wanted whatever happened to happen with a clear head. "Is the artwork that bad?" she teased, instead, and she was glad when Roderick took it in the playful spirit it was intended.

"You'll have to be the judge of that," he laughed. He went into a back room and brought out a chunky sketchbook. They sat down at the couch, thighs just touching, and Addison made herself pay attention to the artwork, not just his sizzling presence beside her. They weren't rushing, she reminded herself. They had all night. They had their whole lives. It wasn't a race.

His art was an eclectic collection of subjects and themes, from comic book heroes and classical life drawings to animals and several pages of Gabby as a baby.

Addison exclaimed over them and turned every page in interest, feeling a little like she was getting to know Roderick with each picture as much as she had in each conversational exchange that they'd shared. Not all of them were successful, and many were barely more than gesture sketches, but all of them had appealing raw energy.

"Could you draw something for me?" it suddenly

occurred to her to ask, looking at gesture sketch of a galloping horse.

Roderick looked wary. "What do you want me to draw?"

"Unicorns," Addison said.

Roderick blew out his breath in relief. "I could probably do that," he agreed.

"What did you think I was going to ask?" Addison had to ask, wild with curiosity.

He squirmed and Addison was reminded again of his proximity. "I thought you'd ask me to draw you," he said sheepishly.

Addison tried to decide how to take that and he saw her confusion and hastily added, "I'm absolutely terrible at making people look like they actually are. I'd give you uneven eyes or too big a nose or a crooked mouth and you wouldn't realize how beautiful I think you are."

"You think I'm beautiful?" Addison could not quite stop herself from asking.

Roderick almost crushed the sketchbook, gathering her into his arms at last, and Addison swiftly rescued it and reached blindly to put it on the coffee table as she tipped back and let him cover her mouth with his.

24

They made out on the couch for a ridiculously long time, until Roderick's mouth was burning and he knew that Addison's must be, too.

He kissed her and kissed her, letting his hands wander all the places he'd been gazing at all evening, the place where shoulder met neck, that place at her side just beyond her breast. Her breast itself, the glorious curve of it, the amazing cup of it in his hand, the way it met her body before her belly. Her thigh, firm and taut, and the way he could follow it to her ass when he pulled her skirt up.

Her hands were no less busy, her mouth no less demanding, and by the time that he had gotten up as high as her underwear—lacy, like she was hoping that he'd get there—and rub a thumb gently over her covered clit, she had gotten his shirt off and was kneading his shoulders like a cat.

"Bedroom?" he suggested.

"Bedroom," she agreed, and he was so happy with her answer that he couldn't let go of her for several moments, kissing her desperately.

He finally made himself roll off of her and draw her up by

the hands, pausing as she kicked off her shoes with a hiss of pleasure, and then leading her back along the hallway towards the bedroom. He stopped to kiss her up against the wall several times.

"Rod," she said, sliding one hand over his cock, and he wasn't sure if it was meant to be a joke, but he didn't care, because she was caressing him through his pants and he could barely even think anymore.

Bedroom, he reminded himself and he caught her hands again so that he could pull her in, glad that he'd tidied up and made the bed, even though neither of them was exactly pausing to appreciate it.

He bent her back over the bed and her legs were up around him as he kissed her neck and tried to figure out how her black dress was attached.

"There's a zipper in the back," she murmured, and that was all the excuse he needed to flip her over.

His brain shorted out a little, her curvy ass pressing back against him as he held onto her hips and forced himself to puzzle out her clothing again. The zipper was tiny and delicate, and he slipped it down as slowly as he could manage, both because he didn't want to damage it and because he wanted to prolong the delicious exposure of her bare back, stroking it as he went.

She whimpered and ground against him. He had to groan and think fixedly about gross grease traps and clogged toilets a moment to calm himself down.

"Condom?" he finally remembered to ask. He'd stocked the bedside table hopefully.

"Implant," she assured him. "It's okay if you don't." Then she added, "But it's nice of you to ask…"

She rolled to face him and the dress fell away from her. Roderick had to unbutton his pants before he merely ripped them off and he wasn't later sure if she removed her undergarments, or if he managed to; he only knew that there was finally nothing between them, nothing but skin and his own hard cock.

They crawled up onto the bed together, kissing again, touching, making small noises of desperation and desire, and then he was in her and they were moving together.

Everything was pleasure and passion, instinct like the sugar sprinkle on a donut that was already decadent. This was where he belonged, buried inside of her, making her rise in ecstasy, her arms around him, her mouth hungry against his. This was where he belonged, making her his, giving her himself, drinking in the touch of her, the heat of her.

When he came, at last, he saw sunspots, and he cried out her name, and he knew that he'd come home.

* * *

They lay together breathlessly for a long time afterward, sweat cooling on their skin as they continued to caress and touch each other in happy exhaustion.

"You could stay," he said, and to his consternation, Addison went rigid in his arms. "Or I could drive you home," he offered swiftly. "I really don't mind."

She hesitated and then said tentatively, "I'd rather go."

He wanted to hold her forever and never let her out of his arms, but instinct gave a twang of warning. He couldn't force her to stay and he wouldn't want to. "It's no trouble," he said firmly, and he kissed her soundly on the neck. "Want a shower first?"

Addison giggled. "I can't decide which would be worse, going back to Wendy's freshly showered, or smelling like this."

"I like how you smell," Roderick told her, and he turned

his kisses into licks into nibbles until they were tickling and giggling and, inevitably, kissing again.

"I should shower," Addison agreed with a contented sigh.

He showed her the bathroom and the trick with the shower knob.

"Isn't a plumber supposed to have the latest in perfectly working faucets and fixtures?" Addison teased him.

"The cobbler's children are the last to have shoes," Roderick countered.

"Are you going to watch me do this?" Addison asked when he settled on the closed toilet to gaze at her through the steam-frosted door.

"Do you mind?" Roderick asked.

She replied by wiping the steam off suggestively and soaping her breasts.

Roderick was tempted to sketch her. She was so perfectly female, so everything that set him on fire.

But sketching in steamy rooms was hard on paper, and he lacked confidence that he could capture with a pencil that exact way that her back met her ass, the way her arms flowed, the lines of her legs. He satisfied himself with trying to memorize her instead and met her at the door when the shower turned off with a fluffy towel to wrap her in.

He put a kiss on her head and traded places, gratified that she seemed as interested in watching him shower as he'd been in watching her.

"You could do bachelorette parties," she suggested when he emerged. She found him a towel, and they dried each other off with plenty of distraction.

"Addison," Roderick said after she'd gotten dressed and was looking for her shoes.

She looked up with a dreamy smile, holding up her last shoe. "Yes?"

He wanted to ask her to marry him on the spot but

hauled himself back. They were taking it slow, not rushing. He shouldn't declare his love yet, and the idea surprised him, not because he thought that he shouldn't, but because he wanted to.

He loved this beautiful, big-hearted woman to the very bottom of his soul, and it wasn't just the aftermath of their toe-curling sex or the curious tingle of instinct making everything faintly magical.

He simply loved her, from her smile to her nurturing spirit, from her strawberry-blonde hair—it was back into its usual crinkly curls after the shower—to her clever fingertips. This was the woman that would complete his life in a way he'd never even known he needed.

"It can wait," he said. "Let's get you home before curfew."

He left her on Wendy's steps with a lingering kiss and returned to his house, weirdly and unsettlingly quiet with neither his daughter nor his mate.

It isn't home without them, his wolf agreed.

*a*ddison floated into Wendy's house, not even caring that her feet still hurt.

Who even *needed* feet, after Roderick had done *that* to her whole body?

"I guess I don't need to ask how your date went!" Wendy exclaimed, coming out of the kitchen. She was wearing plastic gloves that went up to her elbows and an oversized shirt that had once been white and was now stained in clashing colors.

Addison kicked off her shoes and flopped down on a clear square of the couch. "The steaks were very, very good."

"A date with good *meat* is always a good sign," Wendy said with a wink as she sat down on the footstool across from her. "Why are you home? I didn't expect to see you until morning."

"It was just our third date," Addison protested. She didn't try to deny that she'd enjoyed her *meat*; her hair was still damp. "We're not moving that fast." Were they? Staying a night seemed further, faster than just sex.

"He's not Owen," Wendy reminded her.

Addison felt a flutter in her chest that she recognized as the reservations she was still holding onto. "I know," she said gravely.

"Owen was an asshole," Wendy said frankly.

"He didn't seem like an asshole at first," Addison protested. "He was so nice! Everyone liked him! What if…?"

"Roderick is not Owen," Wendy said firmly. "What does your instinct tell you?"

"You can't understand instinct," Addison snapped. She felt bad at once. "I mean…I don't mean…"

Wendy's mouth went to a thin line. "I'm not a shifter, so I can't understand what it's like to be one," she agreed, her voice carefully neutral. "But I know people a little, and I know you're still hung up on the fact that Owen took you for a ride. He gaslighted you and preyed on your trusting nature and isolated you from your friends and tried to control you, and you got *out*. Don't you let him keep his claws in you after all this time."

Addison looked at her hands. "At least I didn't marry him," she agreed. "Or have kids."

"But are you going to let him keep you from *ever* marrying or having kids? It's been years."

Addison could feel the truth in Wendy's words, the pointed observation. "It's not like Roderick and I are anywhere *near* the point of talking about marriage or having kids," she said defensively. It scared her that she wanted to be. She wanted to settle down to a home of her own, a family. And she wanted that with Roderick and Gabby. Was that yearning confusing her instinct? How much could she trust magic anyway?

Then she remembered, "Gabby's mom is back in town."

Wendy looked thoughtful. "But you're the one who had a date tonight."

That probably meant something. Addison hugged a throw pillow to her chest. "It's late," she said. "I should turn in."

She brushed her teeth and stared at her reflection. She shouldn't have given Wendy a hard time about not being a shifter. It galled her that she was dependent on Wendy's hospitality, she realized. Since Owen, she'd hated having to rely on anyone. It gave them power over her.

But trusting people—the right people—wasn't losing power. She could trust Wendy. She could trust Roderick.

Could she trust instinct?

Wendy was painting in the living room—squeezing paint directly onto her brushes—when Addison came out of the bathroom.

"You know, you're right," Addison told her.

"I'm always right," Wendy teased, no hint of anger or resentment in her voice. Wendy never held onto anything, and Addison envied her that carefree attitude. "What was I right about this time?"

"Roderick isn't Owen."

"Good thing," Wendy scoffed. "The world doesn't need more than one of those. I'm not sure it needed the one, either." She glanced sideways at Addison. "That jerk took you for a ride and then chased you half across the country and it's no wonder you're a little gun shy. No one is going to object if you want to take it slow, least of all Roderick."

"Thanks, Wendy," Addison said sincerely. "For everything."

"Hotel Wendy always has a room for her favorite cousin," Wendy said, putting an abstract scarlet sweep across her canvas. "You're a good roommate. You don't eat too much and you pay your share of groceries. No noisy parties. No pet giraffes."

Addison hugged her from behind, mindful of the wet paint on her brush and hands. "Good night."

"Sleep well," Wendy said cheerfully. "I imagine you've got a lot to dream about!"

Addison settled into her creaking air mattress and stared at the ceiling. Wendy had painted a mural there, a colorful space-scape with shooting stars. One of the nebulae looked a little like a bird on fire.

How much more comfortable would she have been staying the night with Roderick? Was she letting her past keep her from the future she wanted, that her lynx knew was right for her?

She shifted restlessly, listening to the distinct squeak of the air mattress, and after a while, she got up to find a notebook and start writing.

oderick woke up early, to a silent house, and couldn't get back to sleep. He checked his texts. Nothing from Ian. Nothing from Addison. Should he call her? Text her an eggplant or whatever it was that people did these days?

He puttered around in the kitchen, repairing a cabinet door he'd meant to fix for weeks now, checking the expiration dates of the food in the pantry. The quiet made him antsy. Surely Gabriella was chewing on electrical cords or strangling herself with dish towels or ordering pet gorillas on Amazon with his phone, being quiet this long. It was so odd not having her there.

He found music files he hadn't listened to since she'd been born, favorite bands and songs that weren't exactly child-appropriate, and after only a few songs, turned them off and put on a Baby Bop playlist.

He finally decided it was late enough and texted Ian, "I can come to get her any time."

Then he texted Addison, "Thought I'd take Gabby to the Nickel City memorial park, want to join us?"

Addison must have been holding her phone and possibly she fumbled it because the tease of her three dots typing something was on the screen immediately and lasted for so long that Roderick ran out of breath holding it.

Ian answered first. "Feeding her pancakes now. She's eating the blueberries out of them. Ready to go when you are. No rush."

Roderick texted him a hasty thumbs up in reply because Addison answered then as well: "I'd love to! Say wen." A second text followed: "When!"

Roderick dredged his mind for a clever reply. "When!" seemed too flippant. And maybe it would look like he was trying to correct her typo when she already had? "Picnic lunch at noon?" he suggested. It was already mid-morning, which would give him time to fetch Gabby and pack a basket.

"Sure! See you at the swings!"

He did not actually have a basket, but an insulated membership warehouse bag would do, and it had room for a few extra diapers and wipes, plus some ice packs and cold drinks. He made sandwiches in every flavor he had ingredients for, tossed in some squeeze applesauce and milk in a covered sippy cup for Gabby. And blueberries, of course.

He completely forgot about Dana until he got her text alert. He slapped the sandwich he was working on together and dived for the phone, heart in his throat. At first, there was only disappointment that it wasn't from Addison.

"Would like to see you and Gabby again," Dana wrote, with a sideways smiley face.

Was he wrong about her intentions? It was so hard to tell through a text, and instinct was no help right now.

He'd been clear with her that he wasn't interested in getting together, though he hadn't been sure what to tell her about Addison beyond a super vague 'I'm seeing someone.'

He certainly couldn't explain to her about instinct; she didn't even know about shifters.

After a moment, he decided not to answer Dana. Not right away. He wasn't at her beck and call. He put the sandwiches in baggies and tucked them into the chilled bag, then sighed and tapped out a reply. "Busy today." Too brief? He didn't want to be too encouraging, so he decided it was good enough and sent it.

"Ok," was her equally brief reply.

Women were minefields, he decided wryly, and somehow he'd gone from one in his life that he could football-carry to three of them, all of them with expectations he barely understood.

Ian looked like he had survived the babysitting and the night, but just barely. "They slept great until about five AM," he said wryly. "Then we had a disco party, a tea party, a couple of fights over toys, and a fashion show, I think. There was a nap at about nine, so you might be safe until after lunch."

"I owe you," Roderick said sincerely. "I mean, I *really* owe you."

Ian grinned. "*Really*, huh? Well, good for you. Is that Cherry's hire at the day care? Miss Frizzle Poppins?"

Roderick grinned and didn't bother answering.

As fussy as Gabby had been about being left with Lucy and Ian, now she didn't want to leave them. She and Lucy tried to hide behind the couch, their legs sticking out.

"That's okay," Roderick said loudly, going to the door. "I'll go on a picnic by myself with allll the blueberries."

"Gaba ababa eeee!" Gabby gave a squawk of protest and crawled out over Lucy, straight to Roderick to pull herself up on his legs and stretch her free arm up to him.

"I dread the day that blueberries lose their bargaining power," Roderick admitted to Ian as they chuckled, and he gathered up all of Gabby's things and swung her up into his arms.

"Want to go see Teacher Addy at the park?" he teased her.

"Abab," Gabby groused, clearly suspecting that she'd been had.

* * *

Addison was waiting for them on a picnic bench by the baby swings. There was a whole section of the park set aside for younger kids, with fragrant bark under low seesaws and short slides. A train-shaped jungle gym pulled a few platforms with plastic zoo animals on springs that could be ridden.

"I brought lunch," Roderick said, hoisting the overfull bag. "I wasn't sure what you wanted, so I made peanut butter, tuna fish, and turkey with lettuce and tomato."

"You give me the hardest choices!" Addison laughed and when she tipped her face up, Roderick gladly kissed her.

"Oh, but wait," Roderick teased. "I also have plain *and* barbeque chips to choose between."

"The agony!" Addison lamented.

"Ababa," Gabby said firmly. She had her eyes fixed on the giraffe. "Ababa!"

"Would you like to lay out lunch while we say hello to the local wildlife?" Addison offered, opening her hands to Gabby.

Gabby's initial interest in the big square-spotted giraffe swiftly turned to terror when she realized how tall it was and Addison took her instead to the lion, which Gabby was willing to pat and babble to.

Roderick had unpacked the lunch by the time they came back.

"You weren't kidding about the sandwich choices,"

Addison said, sitting beside him with Gabby in her lap. "What should I have, Gabby?"

Gabby reached forward and helpfully handed her a sandwich, pausing to maul it only a little bit before Addison could pluck it away. "Tuna fish! Good choice!"

Roderick took the turkey sandwich and offered a piece to Gabby, who stuffed it in her mouth and then looked at him dubiously. She chewed for a few moments, then reached into her mouth and extracted a piece of lettuce, which she offered back to Roderick. He and Addison laughed, and the lettuce was dropped onto the park bench and fell down to the ground.

That caught the attention of a squirrel, who braved the far end of the picnic table and eyed them warily.

Gabby stretched her hands out and strained against Addison's arm. "Ababa gabby eeeee!"

The squirrel wisely fled.

"That's not Lucy, honey," Roderick told her. "That's just a squirrel."

The rest of the picnic was blissful; it was a sunny day, with just enough of a breeze to keep bugs down. It smelled like late summer grass and pine trees. From across the park, older kids were noisily playing on the taller equipment and a few teenagers were pushing each other on the merry-go-round.

Gabby was not terribly hungry. She grudgingly ate a few bites of each of their sandwiches, then they let her down to play in the bark chips and skootch around the picnic table holding onto the bench. She didn't offer to let go and walk free-standing.

"I shouldn't be concerned that she's not walking yet, should I?" Roderick couldn't help asking.

Addison smiled knowingly. "Not in the slightest. Kids get to these milestones when they're ready, and walking late doesn't seem to have even a tiny impact on how they do later in life. I'd guess she's close, just look at her thinking about it!"

Roderick said sheepishly, "I see Amy cruising around, and she's younger."

Addison nodded. "Amy's also shifting already, she's got precocious gross motor skills, but she doesn't make a lot of sounds yet, and she hasn't mastered the same fine motor skills that Gabby has. Have you ever seen a dog try to get a whole pile of tennis balls in their mouth at once?"

Roderick had to laugh at the mental image.

"Kids are like that," Addison explained. "They're trying to hold onto all those tennis balls of skills, and they'll eventually master them all, but if they try to do them all at *once*, they'll just end up chasing them all endlessly. Gabby's doing great. I'm not the slightest bit concerned. One of these days she's just going to take off. You'll forget you were ever worried and wonder why you wanted to hit this milestone in the first place."

Roderick bumped her shoulder with his, grateful. "See, you should be writing those parenting books. The slobbery dog with a mouthful of balls is an image that is always going to stick with me."

Addison shuddered dramatically. "My books couldn't be worse than some of what's out there," she agreed. "Speaking of books, though, I wanted to talk to you about that project I had in mind."

They spent several hours at the park, putting their heads together over Addison's notes and playing with Gabby on the equipment. The toddler was full of mixed feelings about the swings, tolerated being held on the seesaw, and was completely unwilling to let go of Roderick to slide down the short slide, no matter how they tried to coax her.

Her eye-rubbing need for an afternoon nap finally broke up the party.

"She usually sleeps for about forty-five minutes in the afternoon," Roderick told her as they gathered everything up and convinced Gabby they weren't abandoning Lucy the squirrel in the park. "Care to come over…?"

"I promised Wendy I'd help her transplant some peonies later this afternoon," Addison said regretfully. "But maybe tomorrow?"

Roderick winced, remembering Dana again for the first time since he'd brushed her off.

Addison was watching his face as he strapped Gabby into the car seat, and Roderick wasn't sure if her instinct made her guess, "Dana?"

Roderick frowned. "I'd rather see you," he said firmly, shutting the door on Gabby's squirrel-centered protests.

"It's not one or the other," Addison said gently. "You've got business to discuss, it's much more important that you settle…whatever needs settling. Text me if you're free in the afternoon, but I'm not an obligation. I'm not going to be jealous."

"You could never be an obligation," Roderick said sincerely. "I'll text you."

The following day, however, followed another largely sleepless night, and an hour-long screaming fit that meant Roderick scrubbed plans with both Dana and Addison, being vague with the former and honest with the latter: *Have lost my mind and haven't slept. Daughter possessed by demons apparently. We're taking a quiet day.*

She texted back with a heart emoji that Roderick tried not to read too much into.

No one had said anything about love.

27

The front door chime buzzed and Addison deftly fished her phone from her pocket, baby Shane in one arm and a cat tantalizer in the other; she was playing with several of the shifter kids practicing catch and chase dexterity in their animal forms.

Roderick was at the door, distorted by the camera but absolutely unmistakable. Just as Addison's heart leaped in her chest and her fingers reached for the unlock button, a strange woman walked up to him on the sidewalk and began talking to him. Addison wasn't quite swift enough in recognizing the danger to stop her own finger, and the door buzzed open.

Addison's lungs froze at their body posture. Roderick went as tense as a stalking wolf and the woman looked strung as tightly as a bear trap. Her accidental buzz had not gone unnoticed. Even without sound on her phone, it was obvious that the woman was asking to go in, and pointing out that the door had been unlocked. Roderick shook his head and set himself firmly in her way.

Addison swiftly did a headcount of the kids, assessing the

danger. Most of them were in human form, but Jennifer was napping as a puppy and Robert and Gil looked dangerously near having a fight; shifting accidentally was most likely to happen when emotions were running high. They couldn't risk having someone in who didn't know the shifter secret.

It must be Dana, she realized, and she caught herself glaring at the woman's handsome profile. Addison had told Roderick that she wasn't jealous, but she hadn't realized that Dana would be so pretty and fashionable. She looked like she'd just stepped out of a salon. Addison had already been spit up on twice that day and Tara had spent some time 'styling' her hair.

Adrenaline surged in her veins, but none of it was instinct, Addison realized. She was alarmed, and jealous, and worried that she'd screwed up by buzzing the door open with a stranger nearby, but instinct wasn't one of the many emotions surging through her. She didn't have a danger sense, even though the situation certainly warranted one.

You could have warned me, she snapped at her lynx.

Her lynx only gave her an impression of pointedly grooming.

Addison got Shane down in a crib and after talking with Roderick a little longer, Dana finally left. Addison breathed a sigh of relief and unlocked the door again. Only after she had buzzed it open did she realize that it would be obvious that she'd been watching.

She went to meet Roderick at the gate with Gabby walking in front of her holding onto her hands. She stopped a little ways away, to give Gabby a chance to take steps on her own if she wanted to—she knew how much Roderick would enjoy seeing the moment!—but Gabby stubbornly fell down on all fours and crawled the final distance, babbling happily.

Roderick gave her a big smile and swept her into his arms for a hug, then sobered, looking at Addison.

"I told her about you," he said.

What did he tell her? Addison was wild with curiosity. Did he make her out to be his girlfriend? *Was* she his girlfriend? They hadn't really talked about it.

But maybe they should.

"What, exactly, did you tell her?"

"I told her that I was seeing you, that I was seeing you *seriously.* And that this wasn't how I wanted the two of you to meet. It was all I could think of to explain why she couldn't come in while I got Gabby."

Seriously.

The word made her heart sing.

Addison wasn't sure what her face showed, but it must have concerned Roderick.

"I've been wanting to talk to you about this," he said. "About us."

Gabby patted his cheek. "Gaba aba baba," she said firmly.

"About all of us," Roderick agreed. "Addison, I know we said we weren't going to rush…"

The door behind him buzzed. Addison swiftly checked her phone. "It's Amy's mom," she said apologetically. "Shea's coming tomorrow, why don't we have lunch, the four of us?"

"With *Dana?*"

"I can't exactly invite her in here," Addison said practically. "Your place won't feel like neutral ground, and Wendy's would be…oh gosh, just no. If we're all going to be a part of Gabby's life, I should meet her, we should talk about what that's going to look like. Right?"

Roderick looked at her like she'd just hung stars in the sky. "Right," he agreed, a slow smile blooming over his face. "I'll text her and arrange something."

The door buzzed again, as Amy's mom got impatient, and

she heard Cherry call from the playroom, "I got it!" and the door unlocked.

Roderick gathered up Gabby's things, then paused at the door long enough that Addison wondered if she should hop over the gate and give him a parting kiss.

The moment passed before she could seize it and she went to get Amy ready to go.

28

"Well," Roderick said with forced humor as he sat down at the table with their order number on a stick. "Here are all the women in my life in one place."

He winced, wondering if he should have worded it differently, but Addison didn't look offended, and Dana only looked a little skeptical, like she wasn't sure if she should laugh.

Gabby pounded her sippy cup on the tray in approval. "Ababba bee!"

If anyone had told him two weeks ago that he would agree to have lunch out with his fourteen-month daughter, her estranged mother, and his new maybe-girlfriend, Roderick would have doubted their sanity.

It had been Addison's idea, and he reluctantly decided that it was sensible. If Dana was going to be any part of Gabby's life, she was going to have to accept Addison's role in it, even if Roderick and Addison were still figuring out exactly what that was themselves. Gabby wouldn't understand their conversation, but she was the perfect neutral companion: a distracting element who was perfectly happy to be the center of their attention.

The fast-food restaurant at the edge of town, Burger-Z, was safe neutral ground; Roderick hadn't wanted to taint his enjoyment of Heads Up Cafe in case this meeting went terribly, terribly sideways, and the fast food chain had booths that were deep and private.

But he needn't have worried. Both Addison and Dana were both clearly determined to make the best of the meeting; they shook hands and smiled at each other from the beginning. His wolf gave a snuffle of amusement at his concern, content that things were happening exactly as they should. His instinct gave him no warnings even though logic told him this could be a very fraught lunch.

"I understand you're new to Nickel City," Dana said across the table to Addison. It could have been a slight, reminding her how new her relationship with Roderick was, but to his relief, Addison didn't seem to take it that way.

"Yes, I just moved from Buffalo, New York."

Dana whistled. "That's quite a change."

"I was looking for a change," Addison agreed mildly. "I just didn't realize how much of a change it would be." She cast a quick glance his way and blushed a little. Roderick considered taking her hand but thought that it might look too pointed.

"You work at the new day care that Gabby goes to?" Dana continued easily.

"Yes. Before that, I was a private nanny for a couple in New York."

Was Addison trying to prove her qualifications for taking care of Gabby over Gabby's own mother? Roderick had not realized what a minefield common topics could be, and he wondered how to tell her that she didn't have to prove anything, not to him, and not to Dana.

No one asked if Dana was staying long and they skirted politely around the topic of Addison and Roderick's relationship. They talked at length about Gabby, her antics at day care, Roderick's tribulations as a single dad, and his plumbing work. "So I pulled a red glove out of this drainpipe, and that's a little unusual, but not all that unexpected. But two weeks later, a second red glove, clogging up the inlet to a septic tank across town. What are the chances? It's eerie, is what it is."

He wasn't sure when he actually took Addison's hand, or if she had taken his, but he had to let go of her when their order arrived.

That led the conversation casually to food and Gabby added her own bubbly opinions of the meal and the company.

The topic went back to employment, and to Dana's advertising work. "My most lucrative work is for toothpaste companies," she said with a laugh. "If you ever need free samples, hit me up. But I also do public relations for nonprofits and charities. I did some of the advertising for Nickel City's tourist board when I was...last here."

She didn't have to explain what had happened the last time she was here, and Addison swiftly gave a forced laugh and observed, "It certainly was effective advertising. It's hard to find parking in town, and I'm still trying to find a place to rent."

For a moment, Roderick feared that the lunch was going to turn hostile, but Dana seemed as invested in making sure that things went smoothly as Addison was. "I'm staying at the Gold Mine hotel and they've got a lot of vacant rooms, but I've noticed that there are a lot of tourists. I guess most people are renting houses? I talked with the hotel owner for a while this morning. Grace, I think. She's quite a character. Lots of strong opinions."

"There's an assembly meeting on that topic next week," Addison said, suddenly snapping her fingers. "Something about adding some restrictions for short-term rentals and applying a rent freeze. Wendy—that's my cousin, I'm staying with her until I can find a place–she gave me a flyer. I was going to ask you if you planned to go to it, Roderick."

Dana glanced between them curiously—had she thought that Addison was living with him?

"I'd like to go," Roderick said. "I got the flyer, too. But the meeting runs through Gabby's dinner and bath time and I'm sure it will be a long one. Residents are pretty riled up it, and I'd like to weigh in. They're taking written testimony, and I figured I'd send some, but I always wonder how seriously they take it. To be honest, I imagine it's going to be quite a show and I'm sorry to miss it."

"It sounds like a major Nickel City event," Addison agreed. "I'd love to go just to people-watch."

The downside to sitting next to Addison was that it put him across the booth from Dana, and Roderick was trying hard to balance not staring at her and not pointedly looking away from her. He'd rather be gazing at Addison. But in that case, he'd be seated next to Dana, and that didn't seem any more correct. And the only other choice was to put both of them sitting together across from him like he was in a bachelor game show.

So he was watching Dana's face when he mentioned wanting to attend the meeting, and he saw the thought occur to her as she spoke. "I could watch Gabby."

Roderick and Addison went quiet. Gabby tried to fill the silence with her babble, excitedly eating the chicken nuggets on her tray at the same time with very mixed results and a spray of breading.

Dana seemed to recognize that she was taking a risk with the offer, and she quickly added, "I don't mean to assume that you'd trust me. I know that's a lot to ask. I'm sure it's too soon."

Roderick still didn't speak, conferring with his wolf curiously. His instinct was quiet, suggesting that there was no major risk. Dana would care for her daughter, and he didn't have to worry that she would run off with her or try to stake some kind of claim on her.

Without thinking about how it might appear, he turned to look at Addison, wondering what her instinct would tell her.

She met his eyes thoughtfully and Roderick tried to read what was there. She didn't look particularly worried, just intrigued. She glanced at Gabby, who was already getting bored with eating chicken nuggets and was just playing with them making various noises that weren't quite syllables.

"Does she know a lot of words?" Dana asked quickly into the silence that was beginning to feel tense.

"She says a lot," Roderick said, "but I'm not sure how much of it counts as real words. She has some animal sounds that she makes."

"Addy!" Gabby said, but she didn't look at Addison when she said it, so it might have meant anything.

"She understands a lot more than she can say, and she'll burst into real words before you know it," Addison said knowingly. "And then sentences, and then you'll wonder if she will ever stop talking, ever once, for a moment."

"Abababa gabba."

Everyone laughed, but Roderick could feel the underlying tension at the table. Dana thought she'd overreached and Roderick wasn't sure how to assure her that she hadn't. Addison wasn't sure if she should offer opinions on the subject. No one was exactly sure where they fit. Except for Gabby, who knew she was the center of all the attention and loved it. He wasn't surprised when she started fussing. "I suspect that someone needs a new diaper. We'll be back."

Roderick was glad that Nickel City was progressive enough to have changing tables in men's rooms at restaurants; he could only imagine how challenging it would have been for a single dad when he was a kid. He gathered Gabby from the high chair and picked up her bag. She shrieked and, although it was a happy shriek, they were still the object of a fair amount of attention as he carried her away from Dana and Addison, not sure which of all of them he felt sorry for.

"Sorry that this is so complicated, kid," he told Gabby after he had swabbed the table down one-handed and laid her down onto it.

She was cooperative for the changing, cheerfully holding her clean diaper for him and gravely commenting on the decor of the bathroom. "Tuh-tuh!" she said, pointing at a car.

"I want you to have a chance to know your mom," Roderick told her seriously as he got the wet diaper wrapped up on itself and took the clean diaper from her to unfold.

"I think it's important that you know who she is, and it's not the right thing to do to cut her out of your life. I know that she thought she didn't want you, but I can't really blame her for being scared, or for realizing later that she was wrong about it. We've all made mistakes along the way."

"Ha ha!" Gabby agreed.

Roderick smiled down at her. "My future is with Addison, honey, instinct knows. I'm not going to lose her, and I'm not sure how to make her understand that I'm not picking Dana over her by letting Dana see you. And now I have to decide if I'm comfortable having her watch you all by herself. Instinct says you'll be fine, but she's never been around kids, will she know what to do? You can be a handful, sweetheart, and you're nearly ready for your next big milestone."

She tingled to his senses, but only faintly, and his instinct wasn't warning him to whisk her safely home. Wouldn't it? He wrapped the new diaper around her, snugging the tabs around her waist and checking around her legs for any folds or wrinkles.

She giggled and kicked playfully. "Let's get you dressed, squirt," Roderick told her, trying to tuck a leg back into the leg of her pants. "One thing you can count on," he continued warmly, "I will always be your dad, and having two moms around isn't the worst thing in the world."

Then, to his chagrin, there was the sound of a flushing toilet from the single stall that he hadn't thought to verify was empty.

The gray-haired man who came out as he was trying to get Gabby's second leg into her pants looked as embarrassed as he felt, and they exchanged a sheepish smile. He wasn't a shifter, or Roderick would have sensed him, and Roderick cast back over his one-sided conversation with Gabby, hoping he hadn't said anything too incriminating.

"Pretty deep thoughts for a men's room in Burger-Z," the man said with a chuckle. "But she's a good listener."

"Gabba babba," Gabby agreed.

"You follow that instinct, son," the man said, alarming Roderick. But he didn't seem to give the term any unnecessary weight. "And keep taking care of that precious little thing."

"She'll always be the first lady in my life," Roderick agreed.

Follow that instinct, son.

He was a human. It probably didn't mean anything.

29

———

Addy eyed Dana over the table and caught Dana eying her back. They pretended neither of them noticed the awkwardness, and Addy tried to prod her instinct into revealing...anything.

There was no sense of warning from her shifter magic, but no encouragement, either, which meant all she had to go on were her general impressions of Dana. Between Roderick's story and this brief meeting, Dana seemed to be driven, self-sufficient, and capable, but she was also forthright, and she seemed shaken and subdued.

Addy knew herself: she was a sucker for a story of grief. Owen had a compelling story of loss, too, and her sympathy for him had overwhelmed the warnings of her instinct. Well, that and her attraction.

But she didn't feel like she and Roderick were being played by Dana.

"This must be kind of weird," she said sympathetically when Roderick had taken Gabby to the bathroom, drawing all the eyes in the restaurant with their loud and adorable progress.

Dana gave a little snort of laughter. "'Kind of' doesn't even cover it." She chased the last of her drink with her straw and then went on. "I honestly thought I knew what I was doing when I walked away. I felt like *I* was the martyr, giving up nearly a year of my life. And I...just had no idea."

Addy refrained from reaching across the table to her. "It would have been so big and scary," she said, only thinking after she said it that she sounded like she was talking to one of the kids at the day care. Would Dana think it was insulting? "I mean, a baby is a lot." She wasn't helping, she feared, and she wasn't good at grown-up talks, even if she could carry on very long and meaningful conversations about socks and cupcakes.

"Roderick's done really well at it." Addy could hear the hitch in Dana's low voice. "And I'm glad I got to meet you. Gabby is a lucky girl, and I'm...really happy that she'll have such a great family."

The idea tripped Addy up.

A family. *Her* family.

She had thought about Roderick in that way, of course she had, but she'd been so careful to keep it one slow step at a time that she forgot to look at the finish line.

A family. The two of them together with Gabby.

Instinct swelled in her like music. That was the direction of her happiness.

"You don't have to worry about me," Dana said, oblivious to Addy's realization. "I won't try to get the papers changed or anything. I'll leave. I just had to see her, I guess, to know for sure that she was okay and I hadn't ruined her life. I thought maybe I could make it up to her somehow, or rescue her, but it turns out that me leaving was the best thing I could have done for her after all."

"She's in good hands," Addison agreed. Then she worried that it had come out wrong. "I don't mean mine, I mean

Roderick's. I…to be honest, you caught us at a really weird point. We haven't been dating long, and we're still figuring out how we work together."

"I didn't mean to complicate things," Dana said firmly.

"I think it's just generally complicated," Addison chuckled. "But we'll figure it all out, the best way for Gabby, and…" Would it be too ridiculous of her to hope they could be friends? Was it too trusting and naïve of her? Magic wasn't giving her any help, but it rarely did unless the case was extreme.

Roderick returned with Gabby then, and all of them apologetically realized that they had places to be. Roderick had a plumbing appointment and Dana was meeting a girlfriend for coffee.

"Gabby and I have a nap time to attend," Addison said cheerfully. She wondered if Dana didn't think she was utterly inane, then wondered why she cared.

She carried Gabby out to Roderick's car and buckled her in while he talked solemnly with Dana at her car. She wasn't trying to watch them, but she saw them shake hands as they parted. Would it have been a casual embrace if she hadn't been there? Or something more?

Instinct gave a curious little twinge that wasn't warning, almost as if it was laughing at her insecurity.

30

"I've never been to anything *like* this," Addison confessed to Roderick several nights later at the assembly meeting. "Does it happen a lot in Nickel City?"

"This is kind of a big deal," Roderick said. "Most meetings have a couple of outraged people and a few gossips with nothing better to do. This is quite a turnout. Maybe the webpage helped?"

Addison and Roderick had put together a simple webpage called "Neighborhoods for Neighbors" laying out the issue and then posted the link on local social media. Roderick had designed a few graphics for it and Wendy had shared it with an entire army of local artists who had taken it viral.

The courthouse/conference room/community center was crowded, with every seat taken and the aisles filled with standing people. Addison's senses tingled; a surprising number of the citizens who had shown up were magic of some kind, she could tell, and the room was roughly divided; the shifters clustered together to one side and the humans filling the rest of the room, with only a few exceptions.

She recognized some people, Roderick said hello to many

more. They crowded together behind the last row of seats in the shifter corner. A few of them had signs that said, "Neighborhoods for Neighbors."

As the meeting was called to order and people began to step forward and offer testimony, it became clear that the divide in the room was more than just magical.

The human side was against the legislation, almost entirely. Business owners cited the upswing in tourist trade as an economic boom that benefited everyone, realtors complained that they would lose their pending sales, landlords made swift, sometimes sideways complaints about how much new legislation would complicate their business, and what a hardship it would be for them.

The shifter side couldn't lobby directly for keeping their privacy for protecting their secrets, but there were several heartfelt statements about how neighborhoods should remain neighborhoods, how they felt unsafe with strangers perpetually driving into their cul de sacs, and how the visitors sometimes had large, unregulated parties, which called out local sheriffs. One of the speakers brought up the topic of increased theft, as the short-term rentals became a target of petty criminals and put nearby houses at risk as well. There were many glares to the far side of the room as people spoke passionately about being evicted from their houses and unable to find affordable options within an easy commute of their work and schools while the landlords who had spoken earlier looked stony and unforgiving. A few looked guilty but stubborn.

The testimony went on for several hours with no break, and Addison felt sorry for the assembly members, who were mostly human with just two shifters among them. They were all yelled at by both parties and struggled to keep the statements short and focused on the topic. At one point, she thought that two older men were going to come to blows over a property dispute that had exactly nothing to do with short-term rentals or lease regulations.

Roderick took a turn at the little table facing the assemblymen.

"I'm not saying that people don't need to make a living," he said, with a polite nod in general at the human side. "But there are ways to do things that are good for us all long term, and there are ways that aren't. We all rise together, and if we're squeezing solid citizens out in favor of riding a popularity bubble, we'll all suffer together when it pops. I think that the rental restrictions are smart and I want to keep my neighbors."

He received a smattering of applause and a few derisive laughs.

The assembly got more proactive about cutting people off when they got to their time limit. Addison wondered if she imagined their willingness to cut off the people in favor of restrictions more than the landlords and realtors, and eventually, they declared the meeting finished and invited citizens to submit further testimony by mail or email.

"I don't think it went very well," Addison said in disappointment when they left the building at last.

"Veronica has many...well, I don't know if I can call them friends," Roderick said unhappily. "She has a lot of influence here, owns a lot of property. It wouldn't surprise me that she has an assemblyman or two in her pocket, too."

"Do you think the webpage got them worried?" Addison asked.

"They seemed pretty organized," Roderick said thoughtfully. "Maybe it scared them a little."

"Why are there so many of...us...here?" Addison asked as she walked with Roderick to his truck. It was nearly dark now, the sun casting just a smudge of light in the sky, and they had parked quite far from the city center due to tourist traffic that had mostly dispersed.

Roderick unlocked the truck and considered her thoughtfully. "You ever notice how there are lots of trees around here?"

It had become normal at some point, Addison realized. Most of the trees in her neighborhood in Buffalo had been in straight lines or carefully enclosed in iron grates to prevent vandalism.

Here, however, the trees were everywhere. Streets meandered in organic lines around stands of them, as if the town itself were the afterthought to the forest. There was no yard that didn't have several stately guardians.

"I figured that's just how Montana was," she admitted. "Trees and cowboys and state parks."

"This is a pretty special place," Roderick explained. "That famous tree out by Belle Lake is a dryad, Isadora Larix, and this is her forest."

Addison stood with her jaw dropped, staring around at the trees.

It made a certain amount of sense. That tingling feeling of belonging that was like shifter recognition, but not. That alive sensation she'd gotten the moment she drove into town. She thought at first that it was just the difference between a city and a small town with room for yards and gardens, but she'd been to other places with plants that felt nothing like this. Later, she thought it was her shifter instinct, because Roderick was here and he was the key to so much possible happiness.

"What a wonderful thing," she said in awe. "Does everyone know?"

"Not a lot of people, no," Roderick said. "My mother was told by a friend of hers who says that all the Tree City USAs are run by dryads. It's why Arbor Day is such a big deal here."

Addison laughed in delight and clapped her hands. "Every time I think that Nickel City can't get better," she said happily. She sobered to remember that she might not be able to stay if Cherry couldn't afford both the rent and her salary. She had unconsciously hoped that this meeting would solve all of her problems and magically fix the housing market that felt like her last obstacle to complete happiness.

Roderick opened the passenger door for her, and Addison thought that he was going to lift her up into the truck, but he paused with his hands at her waist and bent to kiss her instead.

It was challenging, finding time to be together that coincided with Gabby's naps or bedtime, without inconveniencing Wendy, who slept lightly and had to be up early, so despite several attempts to repeat their third date, Addison had to be satisfied with lingering kisses.

She thought this would be another of those, until Roderick pointed out, "I told Dana the meeting might run really late. She's not expecting us back just yet."

"The assembly did a pretty good job of keeping it short, considering," Addison said breathlessly against his mouth.

"We could go somewhere…" Rod suggested.

"A hotel?" Addison asked, drawing back in surprise.

"I was thinking the Lake Belle overlook," he chuckled. "But I could be persuaded…"

"Your truck is roomy," Addison said quickly, her disappointment in the results of the meeting turning to anticipation. "And it's a lot less expensive and also we probably won't meet someone you have to pretend not to know."

She didn't have to ask twice. Roderick lifted her into the passenger seat and went swiftly to the driver's seat. He'd barely parked at the overlook before their seatbelts were off and they were reaching for each other.

The truck wasn't quite as spacious as Addison had hoped; the passenger seat didn't slide back all the way because of Gabby's car seat, and the toddler's things occupied most of the bench seat in back.

But the console between the two bucket seats flipped up to reveal a narrow center seat, and Addison didn't care that there was a teething ring underneath her when Roderick got his pants down and her skirt up and they were finally, desperately, moving together.

He held her close, filling her in a way that made her whole body respond with joy and eagerness. She felt wild and fierce, and when her pleasure seemed too keen to bear, he took her higher, to bliss and release.

Best of all, it didn't ebb away to shame or regret afterward, but to pleasant contentment, her instinct humming in delight.

31

*R*oderick had some reservations about the idea of going straight home to see the mother of his daughter after passionate (and slightly uncomfortable) truck sex with Addison, but there wasn't much of a way around that unless he stopped at Wendy's to shower...and that sounded more awkward yet.

Addison was running her fingers through her hair as they pulled up, and she checked her reflection in the sun visor mirror briefly, then exchanged a rueful smile with Roderick. "I probably shouldn't care," she said.

"How about my hair?" Roderick asked teasingly. "Did I muss it?"

"Let me check," Addison said gravely and finger-combed his curls vigorously until Roderick was sure they were all standing straight out in a short Afro. "That's better," she said breezily.

He kissed her and they laughed and Roderick felt utterly and completely content. This was how it ought to be, his mate at his side, coming home to Gabby after advocating for their neighbors...even if it had been futile. Of course, it wasn't Addison's home officially, yet, but after Dana left, he planned to ask her to stay the night.

Not for sex necessarily—though he wasn't averse to another round—but he wanted to hold her, sleep beside her, wake up with her easily in his arms, cook her breakfast. Maybe Gabby would sleep in a bit and he could kiss Addy awake and learn more about all her most delicious noises.

They walked to the door hand-in-hand and Roderick put the key into the door. "How do you think Dana did?" he asked before he turned it. "Is Gabby asleep?"

"Dana's capable," Addison said with conviction. "But she also had no idea what she was getting into. I'd give her even odds."

Roderick turned the key. "I told her not to worry if she couldn't get Gabby down, we weren't going to be that late."

But it turned out that they were entirely too late.

Dana was standing in the middle of the living room, her hair wild, her clothing disheveled. There was a look of absolute panic and despair on her face...and she was holding onto a tiny, wriggling wolf pup with gigantic paws who was trying to lick everything in reach.

"I'm sorry!" she wept. "I don't know what happened! She was growling and snapping and then...just...I didn't know what happened!"

"Oh, Gabby!" Roderick exclaimed.

Gabby's head swiveled as she recognized Roderick's voice and she gave a yelp and began to struggle in earnest.

"It's okay, you can let her down," Roderick said.

Bemusedly, Dana obeyed.

Gabby capered directly to Roderick and he bent and scooped her up into his arms, where she changed, giggling, back into human-Gabby, stark naked. "Ababa gabba! Tuh-tuh, aba addy!"

"She is *never* going to learn to walk now," he despaired. "Not when she can run everywhere on four legs."

Addison laughed warmly. "Don't worry," she said, leaning in to kiss Gabby on one of her fat cheeks. "All the shifter children I have raised have learned to walk with two legs, right on schedule, regardless of when they walked with four."

Dana was staring at them with wide eyes and something occurred to Roderick.

He glanced at Addison. "My instinct…"

"Mine didn't warn me, either," Addison observed. "I guess because it's not a problem?"

"Did you know she'd do that?" Dana said in outrage.

"Not tonight," Roderick said quickly. "I wouldn't have left her with you if I'd known. I knew she would soon, but I honestly thought I'd have longer." He'd trusted that he would have warning if Gabby was going to shift.

"Are you...can *you?*"

Some things were just easiest to show. Roderick knelt to put Gabby down on the floor and then flowed down on four paws as a big gray wolf next to her. Gabby grabbed onto the ruff at his neck as her legs swayed and threatened to betray her, then she was a puppy again, romping at his feet. Dana backed into the couch and sat down on the arm of it, staring.

Gabby growled and pounced at his paws, falling over onto her side and rolling back up. Her little whip-tail wagged furiously and she gnawed at his leg.

"You're...a werewolf?"

"Shifters," Addison corrected as Roderick crouched down to lick Gabby and nudge her with his nose, rolling her onto her side when she got rough. "We prefer to call ourselves shifters."

That earned her all of Dana's attention. "Then, you're a...shifter, too?"

Addison nodded serenely. "I'm a lynx, not a wolf. I could show you?"

Dana licked her lips and nodded warily.

Addison put her purse down beside the door and in one smooth move was a lynx. She sat down primly, in every way trying not to look threatening. Roderick sat down as well, his tail wagging. He'd never seen her as a lynx before, and she was simply gorgeous. He wanted to draw her, to capture that soft, plush coat and the big, tufted ears with a pencil. Her yellow-green eyes gazed back fondly.

Gabby, realizing that Roderick was ignoring her now, went to try to play with Addison instead. Addison stepped on her with one of her giant, soft paws and licked her soundly until she turned into a little girl again, squealing in equal parts delight and outrage. Addison shifted, as well, and gathered Gabby into her arms as she stood up.

"Addy!" Gabby said happily. Roderick was beginning to suspect that the sound really did mean Addison and wondered if he should be jealous that she had said it before dada.

Dana slid off the arm of the couch to collapse bonelessly onto the seat cushion next to it. "Well, that's certainly something," she said in wonder.

"Honestly, I didn't mean to spring it on you like this," Roderick said, shifting back into human form and standing. "I knew I'd have to tell you eventually if you were serious about being a part of Gabby's life, but I would have given you a little time first, built up to it."

Gabby reached for him, leaning away from Addison, and he walked over to gather her back into his arms, tossing her a little first. She cuddled happily against him, and he exchanged a knowing look with Addison when she started to rub her eyes and lean her head against him in a clear sign that she was winding down and running out of energy. Early shifts took a lot of steam.

"It's been a big day, little girl," he told her. "Your first shift."

"I'm sorry you missed it," Dana said. "I assume it's a milestone like walking or talking."

"One that they don't mention in most baby books," Addison added with a chuckle.

"No, I don't imagine you could," Dana agreed. She looked a little less stunned now, and she laughed and shook her head.

"Do you want me to put Gabby down?" Addison offered.

Gabby clutched harder at Roderick. "No," he said, "I'll do it."

He walked down the hallway and heard a low hum of conversation rise up behind him when he shut Gabby's bedroom door. He put her in a new diaper and a sleeper, snapping her in and then lifting her back into his arms. He held her like that for a long, peaceful moment, limp and trusting against him as she gradually fell asleep.

Filled to his ears with emotion and gratitude and love, he lay her gently down in the crib. She barely stirred, and he tucked her blanket gently around her and kissed her forehead.

She tugged at his senses.

His little girl was a shifter now, and as much as this complicated his life going forward, Roderick was glad for her and felt like he was made of contentment.

It should have been awkward, being left alone with Dana in Roderick's wake. Addison expected to feel uncomfortable. Threatened, even. Roderick had made a baby with this woman, and Addison herself was still in weird not-committed limbo with him. But instinct told Addison plainly that Dana was no threat. The secret of shifting was safe with her, and she had no designs on Roderick or Gabby.

"Do you want a drink?" Addison offered. "I'm sure Roderick's got something around here."

They ransacked the kitchen and found a liquor cabinet above the fridge, with a bottle of wine and a half-full decanter of fancy-looking single malt whiskey.

"Both," Dana agreed and found glasses in another cabinet.

There was a dining room that looked like it had survived a toddler invasion, and they cleared off half of the table and sat down across from each other.

"So," Addison said, pouring glasses of wine and splashing whiskey unmeasured into the bottom of tumblers.

"So," Dana agreed. "Shifters."

"Shifters," Addison said. She took a sip of the whiskey and shivered and gasped.

Dana downed hers without so much as a wince and Addison gamely gulped the rest of hers down. It burned like fire and she resisted the desire to cough until her eyes watered. "It was probably kind of a shock," she wheezed, clearing her throat. She was such a dork.

"Are there...a lot of you?" Dana wanted to know. "Shifters, I mean?"

Addison still couldn't breathe. "Not many," she choked. "Most of them can drink better than I can."

Dana laughed at that, and Addison gradually got her lungs back under control. When she could smile and talk again, she answered all of Dana's questions.

"It's not werewolf-y like phase of the moon or silver or garlic—no, that's vampires, sorry. We just have an animal companion that we can change shapes with."

"Just one shape, then? Do you want some wine?"

"Yes, please. I should be able to drink that like a civilized person. We each only have one shape. It's genetic, with shifting forms passed from parents to children like hair or eye color. You'll get throwbacks sometimes, a wolf showing up in a line of deer shifters randomly, or an otter in a family of badgers. It usually traces back to that one grandmother no one talks about."

Dana nodded as if that made perfect sense and poured them glasses of wine. "And do you have super strength?" she wanted to know.

"We tend to be a little stronger," Addison explained, taking her glass and sipping it without embarrassing herself again. "But not superhero level feats or anything, just like some people are taller or shorter than others. My senses are a little keener as a human than my cousin's are, but not as good as they are when I'm actually a lynx. Most of my muscles are from slinging children, not from being a shifter."

"That day care Gabby goes to, where you work...it's for shifters, isn't it? That's why Roderick didn't want me coming in."

"You can understand why we have to keep it a secret. And it's especially hard with children who don't know better."

"Are there a lot of day cares for shifters?" Dana asked.

Addison shook her head. "No, not many. Usually, someone has to stay home with shifter children during that age, or a relative watches a few extra kids. I was a nanny for a shifter family. By Kindergarten or first grade, they know how to shift their clothing with them and understand how important it is to keep it all a secret, and babies don't usually shift until they are a year or two old. But I've never seen as many shifters in one town as I've seen here, and there's enough of a market for a full day care. I hope."

Dana nodded thoughtfully. "That makes sense."

They sipped wine in silence for a short time, and Dana finally said, "You said something when you came in tonight, about how your instinct didn't warn you."

Addison considered. "Instinct is hard to explain. I mean, lots of people—humans—have instincts about sketchy people or bad choices. But shifters have that on a different level, warning us of danger, or when to take a chance..." Addison looked up and realized that Roderick was standing in the doorway to the dining room. "Or pointing out a perfect opportunity."

Dana turned and looked at him thoughtfully. "And when we met...?" She looked at her whisky like she regretted saying anything and blamed it.

Roderick took the seat at the end of the table and reached forward to pour himself a shot.

"Instinct isn't an instruction manual or a blinking neon

light. I wanted to believe that everything was straightforward like that, and it never is. But I know you were a part of my ultimate happiness because the magic knew that I wouldn't be complete without Gabby. I wanted to believe that meant we should be together, and I ignored it telling me we shouldn't." He downed the shot and looked at Addison. "And it knows that I wouldn't be complete without Addison."

Addison flushed but didn't try to deny a word of it. It was a constant hum now, familiar and comfortable. She was safe, perfectly where she ought to be. "Instinct knows," she agreed.

"Oh, get a room," Dana said, pretending to gag. Everyone laughed, as she meant them to, but Addison thought there was wistfulness behind her teasing.

They talked late into the night, about shifters, Gabby, the importance of secrecy, and how they would proceed.

"Don't change the papers," Dana said. "I'm already half-crazy for that girl, but she is indisputably yours and I don't want this to turn into a grab for power. You keep custody. You know best how to deal with her, by far. I'll be happy with whatever time you want to share. I don't even know what I'm doing with my life right now. I couldn't be in charge of someone else's."

"She should know you, too," Roderick agreed. At some point during the conversation, they had moved to the living room, and Addison was curled comfortably at his side with her feet tucked up on the couch while Dana sat across from them in an old recliner. "We can make that work if you're going to stay around."

"I think I might," Dana said, as if it surprised her, too. "There's something about this little town that I like. Maybe it's an instinct."

They lapsed into companionable quiet until Dana glanced at her phone. "Oh, gosh, it's really late. I should go." She slipped her shoes back on. "I'm okay to drive home now. Thanks for everything."

Everyone stood, and Addison evaluated her own state. She was tired, but the effects of the whiskey and the smoother glass of wine were long gone. She could drive back to Wendy's, too. She caught Roderick watching her out of the corner of his eye as Dana briskly gathered up her jacket and purse.

They walked her to the door and Addison impulsively gave Dana a swift hug, surprising all of them. Dana was stiff, but Addison thought she looked grateful when she stepped back.

She hung back as Roderick closed the door behind Dana, and the house had one of those moments where everything was weirdly quiet, no fridge running, no heater rattling, a small-town-at-midnight kind of silence outside where a dog barking somewhere blocks away was very loud.

Should she ask to stay? She knew she was still carrying baggage from her past, but if Roderick could be big enough to be friendly with the woman who had abandoned him with their child, couldn't she be big enough to remember that Roderick was not Owen?

Because he was certainly not Owen. He had never done a single thing that made her doubt herself or feel unsafe. He had never played her against anyone else or left her swimming in uncertainty. Her instinct was always in alignment with being with him.

She could gather up her purse and go back to Wendy's prying questions and knowing looks, and he would never question her decision or make her second-guess herself or manipulate her into staying.

Or she could trust him, and trust her instinct, and open her heart to the kind of happiness she had never imagined was possible.

"Do you mind if I stay?" she asked, and Roderick's smile was all the answer she needed.

"I wasn't sure if I should ask," he said, drawing her close. "But I was really hoping."

It was very late, and they had already fed their hunger, somewhat uncomfortably, in the truck, but it was still completely natural to tip her face up and slip her arms around him to kiss him passionately.

If they were going to get undressed for bed, they might as well do it slowly, lingering over one another with plenty of appreciation.

And if they were going to do that, they certainly didn't need to *stop* there. He was hard, and she was wet, and it was a very long time before any actual sleep occurred.

33

*R*oderick woke up feeling like all the pieces of his life had fallen perfectly into place.

Gabriella was making sleepy might-be-waking-up noises over the baby monitor. Addison was peaceful in his arms, all of her curves in all the right places against him. Everything was right in the world and exactly where it ought to be.

Then he remembered the disappointing assembly meeting and frowned, wondering if there was something else he could do to help his neighbors. And...maybe there *was*.

Gabby gave a cry of protest as sleep escaped her at last and Addison stirred and woke. "Oh, good morning," she said, as Roderick sat up. She rolled onto her back and smiled up at him. "I think your little tyrant wants blueberries."

Roderick wanted to insist that Gabby was *their* tyrant, not just his, but he feared that it would be too much to put on Addison at once. He felt like getting her to sleep over was enough of a triumph; he could make himself be patient for whatever else she was willing to commit to.

"What the tyrant wants, the tyrant gets," he said with exaggerated resignation. He kissed her and might have done much more, but Gabby turned her waking complaint into a true five-alarm wail.

"Duty calls," he said, crawling out of bed.

"Duty does," Addison agreed, drawing out the word like she had when they met.

There was a text from Veronica with an imperious request for his service at one of her rentals. Roderick had no problem letting her know that he had other plans. *Sorry. Taking Addison and Gabby to Belle Lake,* he replied. He didn't mind reminding her of her place in his priorities.

"I have an idea," he told Addison over breakfast. Gabby drank her milk and tried to spill it on her tray, banging her sippy cup upside down.

"But is it a *good* idea?" Addison wanted to know.

"I don't know," Roderick admitted. "But I think it's worth a try."

"Well, now I'm dying to know what it is." Addison's eyes always crinkled up when she was joking, and Roderick thought he'd never tire of watching it happen.

"It's about the assembly," he said.

As he'd feared, Addison's face fell as she remembered the disappointing meeting. "It's stupid that I care so much," she said wryly. "I mean I've been here a few weeks. It's just such a nice place and I'm worried that Cherry won't be able to stay in business if Veronica hikes her rent again. I want the day care to succeed. I want this to be a safe town."

"We still have an ace up our sleeve," he said, hoping to bring back the easy joy.

"What's that?" Addison asked plaintively.

"Isadora Larix."

* * *

It was not a second or fourth Thursday, so there was a gate across the private access road that led to Isadora's prize-winning tree. But the gate itself was just a yellow truss on a hinge; there was no lock or cable on it.

"Are you sure this is okay?" Addison asked when Roderick climbed back into the truck after opening the gate.

"I guess we'll find out," Roderick said cheerfully. "My mother always said that you'd never get your heart's desire without actually pursuing it. Instinct only gets you so far without hard work and risk."

"I don't know much about dryads," Addison said, as they drove back to the parking area.

It was a good hike from the truck to the tree, and Roderick wondered if he should have brought Gabby's stroller or a baby carrier. She was starting to be an armful.

"It looks different without a bunch of tourists around it," Addison said.

The whole forest seemed to be sort of coiled in anticipation.

"Isadora?" Roderick called, feeling rather foolish. "Isadora Larix?"

Only the wind answered, and the branches of the monstrous tree rustled.

Gabby got bored in his arms and kicked her legs in frustration. "Abab bee addy."

"Maybe it wasn't such a *good* idea," Roderick conceded.

But as they turned to leave, they found that someone had come out of the forest—or simply appeared—behind them. Addison gave a squeak of surprise and squeezed Roderick's arm.

She was a white-haired woman with a worn, bark-brown face, wearing a simple Native dress of deerskin. Her feet were bare.

"You called?"

"I saw you!" Addison said in astonishment. "When I came to see the tree on my first day here. You were...dressed differently."

Isadora—it had to be her!—sniffed. "I was here for hundreds of years before settlers. I am not constrained to a limited window of human fashion."

"Of course not," Addison said swiftly. "I didn't intend offense."

"None was taken," Isadora said magnanimously. "But I'm sure you didn't call me to discuss clothing trends."

Addison smiled shyly. "I'd honestly love to some time, but no, that's not why we are here." She looked at Roderick.

Isadora smiled back and turned her gaze to Roderick as well. "Alright, then? What do you want?"

Roderick cleared his throat and bounced Gabby in his arms to calm her down. "I don't know how much local politicking you follow, but you may understand that your forest has been a refuge for many of...our kind."

"Shifters, mythics," Isadora said knowingly. "Yes, like is attracted to like."

"Well, progress has been coming to Nickel City recently, and there are conflicts between keeping our town safe and the people who want to develop it. There is...a bill before the local legislation that would give us some protection."

"You want me to interfere in mortal business for these petty little *property* disputes?" Isadora asked, arching one white eyebrow at him skeptically.

"More people and more development mean more incentive to cut down more forest," Roderick pointed out. "A less wild housing market would mean less."

Isadora's lips went tight. "Hm…"

"Ababa," Gabby said, stretching her arms for Isadora.

"A child," Isadora said fondly. "How quaint! And a shifter, too!" She reached for Gabby. "Young things are so odd."

Roderick's arms tightened reflexively, but a careful assessment of his instinct suggested that there was no danger and he let Isadora pluck the child effortlessly into the air and hold her at arm's length.

"Gaba moo eee!" Gabby told her, giggling.

Addison chuckled.

"She makes as much sense as most of you do," Isadora said, returning Gabby after a curious inspection from the distance of her arms.

Then, without any explanation or courtesies, she vanished as suddenly as she had appeared.

"Oooo?" Gabby said, looking around like a dog after an imaginary ball had been thrown.

"Did we get an answer?" Addison asked plaintively after a few moments of silence.

"Not really," Roderick said. "Which probably is our answer."

"It was worth a try," Addison said comfortingly, as she put her arm around his waist. "And it was a beautiful day to come out here."

They walked back to the truck through the forest, hand-in-hand.

"We don't have to go straight back, do we?" Addison asked wistfully. "There's nobody here…"

For a moment, Roderick's mind went very different places, and he wondered what Addison planned to do with Gabby while they—"Oh, you mean we could shift and run around a little?"

Addison smiled like the sun. "When was the last time you had a chance to run around as a wolf in the wilderness?"

Too long, his wolf complained.

Addison stepped back from him and was rather suddenly capering around as a fluffy-furred lynx.

Gabby shrieked in delight, and Roderick only had to tell her once, "Want to be a wolf?"

He had to help extract her from her romper and diaper, because she didn't yet know to think them into her form with her, and a puppy was not nearly the same shape as a toddler. He got her down on the ground, folded her clothing, and left it on the seat of the truck, then he was bounding after his mate and his daughter on four legs.

34

Addison didn't want to think about the fact that they'd lost their last hope for getting the legislation passed that would save neighborhoods for neighbors and, more selfishly, keep Cherry in business so that Addison could keep her job. It wasn't just that she loved the job, and the life she could see unfolding before her. She loved the day care, and the town, and Cherry herself. The future felt murky now; even her instinct felt muted.

It was a pretty day, and she concentrated on how lovely it was, and what fun she could have right now, ignoring all of her misgivings and disappointment.

Gabby was delighted to roll on the forest floor and dig with her giant puppy paws and scamper and growl and chase sticks and tails. For a long while, they all romped, a wolf, a lynx, and a puppy. Gabby got clumsier, after a while, and Addison caught her by the ruff and carried her to a patch of sunlight by the parking lot, curling up around her and licking her as the puppy growled playfully and protested.

Roderick looked like he'd just gotten started and he gave

a sigh, his tail drooping. He turned back into a man and stooped to scratch Gabby's chin.

Addison jerked her own chin in the direction of the forest suggestively, putting one paw protectively over Gabby. *Go run,* she thought at him, purring, wondering if she would have to shift to convey the suggestion. Gabby was comfortably sprawled between her paws now, panting happily.

"You think I should go running?" Roderick asked hopefully.

Addison nodded.

Roderick looked conflicted, then grinned broadly. "Twist my arm," he said joyfully, and then he was bounding away as his long-legged wolf.

Gabby whined and tried to follow, but Addison groomed her firmly and she quickly settled.

Gabby didn't seem interested in sleeping, but she was happy enough to be wrapped in Addison's purring warmth, and she snuggled contentedly.

Addison's keen lynx ears heard the car as far away as the highway, and she expected it to turn away at the gate until she remembered that Roderick had left it open. Still, there was a big sign that said the tree with its plaque was only open on the second and fourth Thursdays, surely they wouldn't come all the way in?

It continued to approach and Addison grew worried. She couldn't just stay here like this, waiting for a stranger to spot a lynx with a wolf puppy. She shifted, gathering Gabby into her arms. "Sweetie, I'm going to need you to be a little girl again. Fingers and feet, like we do at Cherry's, okay? Fingers and feet!"

Gabby had absolutely no interest in being a girl again.

She chewed on the collar of Addison's shirt and wagged her little tail, squirming with renewed energy.

Any moment, a stranger was going to catch them. Could

she pass Gabby off as a domestic puppy? Would she decide to shift at exactly the wrong time? The truck was locked, and the keys were probably safe in Roderick's shifted pocket, so even if she were a little girl, it would be weird that she was a naked little girl.

Then the car turned into the little lot, and Addison realized in horror and hot terror that it wasn't a stranger at all.

She stared at the familiar car as it pulled into the space at the end, opposite from the truck, and she immediately recognized the figure that got out of it.

"Owen."

He hadn't changed a bit. He was still tall and handsome and strode confidently across the lot to her. He didn't interest her the way that he had when they first met—how could he after Roderick? And even though Addison realized, as the shock of seeing him passed, that she wasn't scared of him the way she'd been when she finally left him, she didn't need instinct to warn her of the danger.

"Veronica said you might be here," he said chidingly.

"How do you know Veronica?" Addison asked in astonishment. "And how would she know where I was?"

"I know all the important people, darling," Owen said dismissively. "Apparently her *plumber* knew where you'd be."

Owen said plumber like it was some kind of insult, but Addison could only think that she'd take Roderick the plumber any day over Owen the jerk.

"Addison, honey, what were you thinking?"

"I was thinking I'd be glad not to see you again," Addison said. She was dismayed to find that her voice trembled, and she held Gabby closer to her. "How did you find me?"

"You did a good job staying under the radar," Owen said, his voice that same kind of reasonable snake oil as ever. "But I had a buddy keep an eye out on your social security number, and it looks like you recently got official employment."

It had been perfectly reasonable to give Owen all of her personal information. His reasons had all been completely legitimate, and Addison had ignored the twinge of instinct that suggested she shouldn't. Her job as a nanny had been under the table, so she wouldn't have shown up on his radar until she started working for Cherry. It was the first time that Addison had felt any regret for her new job.

"What do you want?" Addison asked. She did better at keeping her voice moderated that time.

"It's not about what I want," Owen said kindly, "it's about what you want, honey. You know I'll give you anything you need. You can leave this hick town and come back where you belong."

He always thought he knew better than she did about what she needed, and now it was painfully obvious how wrong he was. For a moment, Addison was more outraged by the "hick town" statement than the implication that she needed Owen.

Gabby was squirming for freedom. She wanted to run around again, and Addison worried that she'd struggle herself into human form. She'd never told Owen about being a shifter, not sure how at first, and later grateful for that reluctance to protect her secret. She bounced Gabby. "You're a puppy, you're a puppy," she murmured.

"Cute mutt," Owen said. "Is it house trained? I could let you have a pet if you needed something to nurture."

Addison actually laughed. She couldn't imagine a pet living with Owen. Dirty paw prints? Dog fur? Slobbery kisses? Owen was the exact opposite of that. And she was done with Owen "letting" her do anything.

"I'm not going back with you, Owen," she said firmly. "I'm

not interested in you anymore. You were a jerk and I don't need you."

"There's no reason to exaggerate things," Owen said, in his terrible, suave voice. "I was so generous with you, so understanding. I gave you everything you ever needed."

He was standing uncomfortably close and Addison didn't want to give him the satisfaction of stepping back to get more space between them. "You were a jerk," she repeated firmly. "Get out of my space and get out of my life."

He knew how much his proximity was distressing her, the bastard, and he was enjoying it. "Nice doggy," he said, reaching towards her just to make her flinch back.

Gabby was tired of being held, and she could probably feel all the tension and nervousness in Addison. She took Owen's approach exactly as he'd intended it, and with all the self-control of a frustrated toddler, she surged toward his hand and bit down.

Owen screamed and leaped back, shaking his hand and swearing. Addison wished that she'd thought to bite him first and didn't scold Gabby, hoping fiercely that she'd stay a puppy, just a little bit longer.

Owen had never been violent with her. He'd never needed to, knowing exactly how to undermine her self-esteem and make her question her resolve.

So Addison was caught by surprise when he bent and picked up a thick fallen branch, advancing on her with fury in his eyes.

In her arms, Gabby barked and tried to speak. Addison took a step back in dismay, certain that the little girl was going to try to shift and that Owen might try to hurt her anyway. She had to protect Gabby—and Gabby's secret—at any cost.

35

Roderick thought at first that his anxiousness was from leaving Gabby behind. He always had mixed feelings about letting her out of his sight. But he trusted Addison with his heart and his life, he reminded himself, firmly ignoring the tiny flush of unease.

He just needed to run, to feel the forest floor under his paws and shake loose from his human form for a short time, so he forced himself away from where Addison was distracting Gabby.

And it felt good, letting his wolf stretch, letting his senses expand out ahead of him. He could smell the summer heat in the underbrush. It was cool, beneath the trees, and the soil had a distinct acrid smell to it that felt like home. He didn't follow a trail, just hurtled through the forest, leaping fallen trees and gorges with no particular destination.

When he slowed, near the ridge, all of his reservations came crowding back and he stopped, nose in the air, to listen.

This wasn't merely the nervousness of being away from his child, there was an undercurrent of instinct, strong and true, warning him with increasing volume of danger, risk, threat, MENACE.

Roderick turned back the way he'd come, running twice as fast, faster than a wolf was meant to go, until his lungs were straining, his muscles burning, and his paws aching.

Danger, danger, danger...

It drew him along like an arrow, back on a straighter path than he'd come, until he was bursting out of the thin underbrush like a mad creature, straight to where Addison, in her human form, was trying to shield Gabby, growling and yipping in her wolf form, from a man who had picked up a fallen branch and was advancing on them.

The stranger clearly reconsidered his attack at the approach of a snarling adult wolf but didn't drop his club or step back.

"I always knew you had secrets," he spat at Addison. "You fooled everyone else with your sweet, innocent, too-good-to-be-true facade, but I know what a dirty, trashy hussy you were."

"I wasn't the one doing the lying and manipulating, Owen," Addison said, and her own voice was a low growl.

Owen.

Roderick's impulse to punch Addison's ex had been replaced with a barely restrained desire to tear his throat out.

But Addison, even with her arms full of squirming Gabby, lifted her chin and advanced on him. "I don't need you, I don't want you, and you have no power over me anymore. You are a sad, worthless excuse for a man who didn't have any self-value unless he could dominate someone. I'm not sorry I escaped you, and I hope that I never see you again. You are delusional and weak. I deserved better."

With every word, Owen flinched, his fist around the branch going tense and white. Roderick kept his eyes on his throat, watching for any hint that he was going to attack, prepared to get there first. He was growling and panting...and Gabby suddenly realized he was there and gave a yip of excitement.

Several things happened at once: Owen lifted his limb, Addison turned, protecting Gabby in her arms and shielding her with her body, as the toddler shifted back to her human form, and Roderick charged forward.

Owen staggered back as Roderick leaped at him, snapping strong jaws with sharp teeth around his branch and ripping it from him by force. Owen fell back with a cry of horror and dismay, and Roderick dropped the stick as he straddled him and growled down into the man's stricken face.

Behind him, human Gabby was wailing in distress. Owen looked confused and terrified. Roderick glared down into his face, then deliberately stepped back, giving him space to get up and run.

Owen didn't need a second invitation, scrambling backwards on his hands until he could get up and stagger away, nearly falling before he got to his car. Roderick paced him, snapping his teeth in warning every time he slowed, until the car door slammed with Owen behind the wheel.

Roderick thought for a moment that Owen would try to run him down, and he waited on legs like coiled springs to dodge out of the way, but Owen chose the sensible path and peeled out from the parking lot rather than staying to prolong the conflict.

Once the sound of the car had died away down the access road, Roderick eased back into human form and turned to find Addison standing with a fussy, naked Gabby in her arms.

"I don't think he saw her," she said, her voice shaking like it hadn't once through the entire confrontation.

Roderick gathered them both into his arms, grateful for

that at least, and felt relief surge through him on the heels of the instinct that had driven him back.

If Addison wept while he was holding her tight, she had controlled it by the time he was willing to let her go.

"How did he find you?" Roderick wanted to know.

"Apparently, he knows *Veronica*," Addison said.

That was certainly an unsavory connection to imagine.

"Abba aga gaba wheeee…" Gabby complained.

"We should get Gabby into some clothes," Addison said sensibly. "It's too chilly to be naked, and there are mosquitoes."

Roderick took his daughter and tossed her a few inches in the air to make her shriek in joy. "I bet *that guy* needs a new diaper, too," he said with satisfaction.

Addison laughed so hard that she had to hold on to him.

Tara's mother usually picked her up at exactly the time she said she would, dressed in her nurse's scrubs. She generally resisted efforts to draw her into conversation, though she was always kind and never impatient with Tara or her baby brother Shane.

Addison wasn't going to be brushed off this time, however, and she met Vivian Yang at the gate with something other than her baby.

Vivian looked at the little pile of paper that Addison handed her cautiously, as if she was expecting eviction papers or some kind of summons. "What's this?"

"I wrote this for Tara," Addison said, bursting with excitement and anticipation. "But I wanted you to see it first."

It was all she could do not to squirm as Vivian flipped through every page, reading each one carefully. Her expression was cool and Addison tried not to assume the worst. "Gabby's father, Roderick Douglass, did the artwork for it. He's a plumber, you wouldn't guess he was so good at art, too. He's got a lot of talent, I think. Of course, I'm a little biased."

Babbling, Addison recognized. She was definitely babbling. But Vivian was paging through so agonizingly slowly and Addison was suddenly worried that she had overstepped, or misunderstood, or done something terrible. Should she have done more research? Maybe she had gotten something wrong. Vivian's hands turning the pages were starting to tremble.

To Addison's horror, she started to crumple the page, then lifted her gaze and Addison could see that tears were tracking down her face.

"I'm sorry!" Addison said in dismay. "I didn't mean to—"

"You made this for Tara?" Vivian's voice was full of grief.

"I haven't shown it to her yet," Addison said swiftly. "If you don't like it—"

Vivian gave a sob. "It is beautiful. It is a gift. I have never seen—I have never been—This is—Oh! I have gotten it wet and wrinkled! I am so sorry!" She tried to flatten the pages, still weeping.

"It's just a copy!" Addison was quick to tell her, not sure how to feel yet. "A few of the pages aren't finished yet. Roderick planned to add color to all of them."

"Mama?"

It usually didn't take the kids long to figure out when someone arrived at the day care, and Tara was standing with Gil, who was pulling his shirt on over his head and somehow had gotten both arms in one sleeve. Amy was toddling their direction and Gabby was crawling after, determined not to be left behind.

"Mama, what's wrong?" Tara's thin voice was worried. "Are you sad?"

Vivian cried harder, but she was quick to say, "No, honey, I'm happy, I'm so happy." She stepped over the gate, knelt down, and drew Tara into an embrace with her free arm.

"Teacher Addy just showed me something that she made for you, and I'm so happy!"

Vivian showed her the first pages and Tara looked up at Addison in astonishment. "This looks like...me," she said shyly.

Addison could only nod, or she was going to cry as hard as Tara's mother.

"Will you read it to me?" Tara begged.

"'Cara was a unicorn,'" Vivian read, her voice wavering. "'But she wasn't like the other unicorns who lived in Heart's Hollow. Cara was a kirin—'" she had to stop and pull Tara close, burying her face in her hair.

"It's called *The Kirin who Could,*" Addison said when it looked like Vivian wouldn't be able to continue. "It's all about what a kirin can't do, and about what she *can* do. I don't know if I got it all right. I wanted it to be a surprise, and I didn't know any unicorns to ask. I can fix anything that's wrong, of course, and we'll print you a fresh copy. Just let me know if you want anything changed. I also wasn't sure if it was too close to Tara's name, I can use something else."

"It looks like me," Tara repeated, and she was crying like her mother was, though she looked like she wasn't sure entirely why.

Amy and Gabby had reached them by now, and Amy was so distressed by the tears that she fell over and turned into an owl, peeping and hopping out of her diaper. Not to be left out, Gabby turned into a puppy and squirmed from her clothing to try to play with Amy.

The front door buzzed onto that chaos and Addison swiftly let Roderick in after checking the camera.

Vivian climbed back over the gate with the papers in her hands and fell weeping into his arms, then seemed to collect herself. "Thank you so much, Mr. Douglass. I can't say how much this means—It's so—I can't—!"

Rod, looking a mixture of alarmed and sympathetic, patted her kindly on the back. "Of course, Mrs. Yang. Of course. It was all Addison's idea."

Then Vivian was back to embrace Addison, and Addison really did cry in earnest at that and Tara began to bawl and Gil tried to stand on his head to cheer her up, shouting, "Look at me! LOOK at ME!"

"What on earth is going on?" Cherry demanded, coming from the back room with Shane, who was cooing happily in her arms. "Gil, is that your inside voice?"

Gil fell over, turned into an armadillo, and just as suddenly shifted back and shouted, "I REMEMBERED MY CLOTHES!" in what was very definitely not an inside voice.

Vivian proudly and tearfully showed Cherry the book and Tara crowded in to point out the pictures that looked like her while the other children ooh-ed and aww-ed.

Amy tried to eat the pages.

Everyone wiped their eyes and Vivian said thank you over and over while she gathered up Shane's diaper bag and Tara's backpack.

Addison felt about as tall as a tree and completely wrung out by the time they had gone. Roderick stood beside her and rubbed her back. "Was it everything you hoped it would be?" he asked.

"Even more," Addison said honestly. Her heart felt full.

"You've still got tears on your face," Roderick pointed out, and he used one callused thumb to wipe them away, then leaned down to kiss her cheek.

"Happy tears," Addison promised.

It occurred to her that Owen coming in on such an event would have made her feel stiff and uncomfortable. He would have disapproved of her tears and frowned at the noisy children.

She was getting tired of comparing Roderick to Owen at

every turn. Roderick was a partner and his support was given without strings. Addison didn't even need instinct anymore to tell her that he was safe to love; he had proved it by respecting her at every step of the way.

She was quite sure that the doorbell did not ring, and that no one unlocked the door, but Isadora Larix was suddenly standing in the middle of the daycare, dressed this time in a fine wool suit dress straight out of the fifties, complete with a pillbox hat.

"How quaint," she said, looking around in interest. "The decor is not exactly historically accurate, is it?"

"The kids don't really care," Cherry pointed out. "Can I help you?"

If she was surprised that Isadora had abruptly materialized in the middle of her day care, she didn't say so, and Addison wondered if Cherry knew who—or what—the recluse was. None of the children seemed to find her sudden appearance unusual.

"You're Cherry Aimes?" Isadora stepped forward and offered her hand. She was wearing gloves that matched her suit.

"Ms. Larix," Cherry said politely, answering at least that question. They gravely shook hands.

"I was surprised to hear that there was a day care opening for shifters only," Isadora said without preamble. "I would like to enroll my daughter."

Roderick and Addison exchanged a look that suggested a daughter was news to him, too.

"I presume that she is not a shifter, but that she will have special needs that we can accommodate?" Cherry said without so much as a flutter of surprise, answering that question as well.

"Her range is not very far yet, but her sapling is still small enough to transport easily in a pot," Isadora said. "Otherwise,

I imagine it will be the same consideration you would have for any young creature. Don't expose her to toxins or allow anyone to eat her."

Addison made an ungraceful snort trying to hold in her laughter.

She had composed her face, barely, by the time that Isadora glanced at her.

"Of course not," Addison agreed. "We discourage the children from eating each other."

"Very well," Isadora said. "Let us discuss payment."

"I have a fee schedule printed," Cherry said, starting to turn back to her office.

"I do not deal with mortal money," Isadora scoffed. "And I am doubtful that you would contract for sexual favors."

Addison's second attempt to hold in her laugh was even less successful than the first and Roderick made a choked noise at her side.

Cherry raised an eyebrow. "That is not a part of my usual business plan," she said very carefully.

"I came prepared to bargain," Isadora said, apparently not taking notice or care for their discomfort. "I understand that there is a resolution before the assembly that you have a particular interest in."

Everyone sobered.

"Yes," Cherry said slowly. "It would prevent rent increases above a certain rate. It...could mean the difference between continuing the day care and having to close it."

Isadora was nodding impatiently. "Yes, yes, and keep neighborhoods for neighbors. I researched the issue after these two brought it to my attention. I can ensure that it passes if you will allow my daughter to attend your school four days a week for a year. We can negotiate new terms at that time if I find it beneficial to her social development."

Everyone in the room was very quiet in astonishment,

except the children, who were gleefully playing a game with the soft blocks that seemed to involve building walls around Amy, who hopped and squeaked in happy delight because everyone was paying attention to her. Gabby was dismantling the walls as fast as they could be erected and no one seemed to mind.

"How—" Roderick started to ask, then apparently he reconsidered.

Isadora answered anyway. "I have a certain amount of influence with the older citizens of Nickel City, including many who have contributed greatly to individuals with political aspirations. I haven't had a lot of interest in your petty mortal politics, but I do understand how they work after all this time. I can assure you that what I want, I *will* get. Do we have an agreement?"

Cherry looked stunned, and she hesitated. "No one will get hurt?"

Isadora looked affronted. "Of course not. Everyone will walk away convinced that they got exactly what they actually wanted."

Cherry nodded. "I think we have an agreement."

Isadora shook her hand decisively, then brushed at her skirt as if Cherry's hand had been dirty. "Very well. I shall bring my daughter on the first day of next week."

Then she vanished.

"Yes!" Addison pumped her fist in the air and danced around in a little circle.

Roderick felt like it was appropriate to kiss her soundly in celebration. "Veronica Chase is going to chew glass," he said, feeling smug.

"Why would she CHEW GLASS?" Gil wanted to know.

"It's an expression, honey," Cherry said soothingly. "I'm so impressed that you shifted with your clothes on earlier! Can you do it again for me?"

Gil promptly turned into an armadillo and rolled back into the fray with Amy and Gabby.

"Did you ever come up with a name for the day care?" Roderick asked.

"Shea suggested the Gingerbread House," Cherry laughed. "I was afraid that might sound like we ate children. Tater Tots was almost as bad."

"What about Tiny Paws?" Addison suggested.

A moment of silence met the idea. "I like it," Roderick said honestly.

"Yes," Cherry said, looking pleased. "It hints at shifters, without giving it away, and we can put paw prints all over the logo."

There was a buzz at the door, and Addison let Gil's father and Amy's mother in. "Please check for lost socks," she reminded them as they gathered up their things. There were ten small socks pinned to the board now.

Then the day care was quiet, only Gabby remaining. She seemed content to pile the blocks while Addison and Cherry did their rounds of the room, disinfecting and tidying. Roderick sat down with Gabby and helped her stack blocks until they were done.

He could not quite keep himself from watching Addison's happy caper around the room. Every so often, she would spin around, or impulsively hug a stuffed animal for no reason. She was so lithe and beautiful and lively, all of her emotions right there in her light step and beaming face. Seeing her so joyful did something inside of Roderick, made everything feel settled and perfect.

She finished the closing chores for the day care while Cherry retreated to do some bookkeeping and gathered up her own jacket and purse, meeting Roderick and Gabby at the door. Gabby was nodding off on his shoulder.

"Oh my gosh, I'm so relieved," Addison said as she pulled

the door shut and locked it behind her. "Veronica won't be able to raise Cherry's rent unreasonably ever again, and I have some hope that I can keep my job. I wonder how many of those real estate deals are going to fall through now?"

Roderick thought about Ian and the sale of his rental. "I just hope that it isn't too late. Housing prices aren't going to drop immediately. It will take a little while for everything to stabilize back to something reasonable."

"I might have trouble finding a place to rent for months and months," Addison agreed. "Maybe even a year."

Roderick bit back his impulse to offer her his spare room again. He knew quite well why she was reluctant, why she wanted to maintain her independence, and he didn't want to push her too hard or question her autonomy. He respected her boundaries, even while he ached to always have her close.

So he was surprised when she very suddenly said, "Do you want to move in together?"

He'd been thinking about it so hard, reminding himself so firmly not to ask that he stared at her stupidly for several moments.

"We don't have to," Addison said swiftly when he didn't answer. "I just thought...it feels…"

"Instinct," Roderick said because it was humming like a motor between them now.

"It's the right thing, at the right time," Addison said quietly.

Everything seemed to click into place. "Addison Carmichael, will you marry me?"

For a moment he thought he'd gone too far, that instinct had pushed him too fast. He should have been satisfied with having her move in with him.

Then a smile bloomed across her expressive face and she beamed up at him in delight. "I will," she said softly. "I will!"

Roderick wasn't sure if he gathered her into his arms or if she stepped into them, but then they were embracing, Gabby wedged between them.

"I love you," he said to them generally.

The sleepy toddler reached out and patted Addison's cheek. "Addy," she said contentedly.

And everything in the world was right, with instinct singing in satisfaction.

Continue the Nickel City adventures in Dragon's Instinct, or read on for a sneak preview of the first chapter!

A NOTE FROM ELVA

Thank you for picking up Wolf's Instinct! This is a book I wrote from the heart, mostly because I wanted a whole lot of adorable shifter kid hijinks and I write the kinds of books I love best. I hope that you had a nice escape to Nickel City, and I look forward to returning to it in future books.

I would very much appreciate your reviews on Amazon, Goodreads, or Bookbub (follow me at any of the above) if you enjoyed this book! I love to hear from readers, and you are welcome to email me at elvaherself@elvabirch.com with any questions, or if you catch any stray typos…or if you just want to say hi.

To find out about new releases, you can follow me on Amazon, subscribe to my newsletter, or like me on Facebook. You are also welcome to join my Reader's Retreat on Facebook for sneak previews, cut scenes, giveaways, and more—including the book I'm not writing!

~Elva

MORE BY ELVA BIRCH

Want some more extra short stories, including a Shifting Sands Resort ménage? Join my mailing list for sneak previews, extras, bonus stories, and more, or join my Reader's Retreat on Facebook!

* * *

The Royal Dragons of Alaska: A fascinating alternate world where Alaska is ruled by secret dragon shifters. Adventure, romance, and humor! Reluctant royalty, relentless enemies… dogs, camping, and magic! Start with The Dragon Prince of Alaska.

* * *

Lawn Ornament Shifters: The series that was only supposed to be a joke, this is a collection of short, ridiculous romances featuring unusual shifters, myths, and magic. Cross-your-legs funny and full of heart! Start with The Flamingo's Fated Mate!

* * *

Suddenly Shifters: A hilarious series of novellas, serials, and shorts set in the small town of Anders Canyon, where something (in the water?) is making ordinary citizens turn into shifters. Start with Something in the Water! Also available in audio!

* * *

Birch Hearts: An enchanting collection of short stories and novellas. Unconstrained by theme or setting, each short read has romance, magic, and heart, with a satisfying conclusion. And always, the impossible and irresistible. Start with a sampler plate in Prompted 2 for fourteen pieces of sweet-to-sizzling flash fiction, or the novella, Better Half. Breakup is a free story!

* * *

A Day Care for Shifters: A hot new full-length series about adorable shifter kids and their struggling single parents in a town full of mystery and surprise. Start the series with Wolf's Instinct, when Addison comes to Nickel City to take a job at a very special day care and finds a family to belong to. Funny and full of feeling, this is a gentle ice-cream-straight-from-the-container escape. Sweet and sizzling!

WRITING AS ZOE CHANT

Shifting Sands Resort: A complete ten-book series - plus two collections of shorts. This is a sizzling shifter romance set at a tropical island resort. Each book stands alone but connects into a great mystery with a thrilling conclusion. Start with Tropical Tiger Spy or dive in to the Omnibus edition, with all of the novels, short stories, and novellas in my preferred reading order! It's available in audiobook and hardcover. This series crosses over with Fire and Rescue Shifters and Shifter Kingdom!

* * *

Fae Shifter Knights: A complete four-book fantasy portal romp, with cute pets and swoon-worthy knights stuck in a world of wonders like refrigerators and ham sandwiches. Start with Dragon of Glass!

* * *

Green Valley Shifters: A sweet, small town series with single dads, secret shifters, sweet kids, and spinsters. Low-peril and steamy! Standalone books where you can revisit your favorite characters - this series is also complete with six books! Start with Dancing Bearfoot! This series crosses over with **Virtue Shifters**, which starts with Timber Wolf.

BEHIND THE SCENES

What is Patreon?

Patreon is a site where readers and fans can support creators with monthly subscriptions.

At my Patreon, I have tiers with early rough drafts of my books, flash fiction, coloring pages, signed and sketched paperbacks, exclusive swag, original artwork, photographs…and so much more! Every month is a little different, and there is a price for every budget. Patreon allows me to do projects that aren't very commercial and makes my income stream a little less unpredictable. It also gives me a place to connect with my fans!

Come find out what's going on behind the scenes and keep me creating at Patreon! patreon.com/ellenmillion

DRAGON'S INSTINCT - SNEAK PREVIEW!

Shots sizzled across the speeder's bow and Turnkey dove at the controls. "We've got a problem!" he hollered back to the engineer.

"You're telling me!" Tagrin shouted back. "We've got a coolant leak in the quarterdeck and a crack in the second hull! She's not going to hold together long enough to break atmo!"

"I know how to fix this!" Turnkey—

Ian stopped typing, his fingers poised over the laptop.

He had no *idea* how to fix this.

It had taken him twenty minutes to re-read and remember where he was even going with his plot when he sat down to write and his brain felt shattered. He couldn't remember the last time he'd gotten a full night's sleep or more than an hour of writing time in one sitting. Every time that he so much as started feeling like he was making progress on his book, Lucy needed a snack, or a new diaper, or a hug, or a nap, or it was time for a meal or to do laundry or there was a toy that needed to be repaired.

Or, like now, there was suspicious silence, which was even worse.

Ian thought he'd have a little window of writing opportunity. Lucy had been happily playing with her food at the table, and as slow as she ate, Ian guessed he might be able to get a few hundred words written.

He didn't want to think about how a few hundred words at a time wasn't going to get him finished by the publisher's deadline, or how many times he'd had to delete big chunks because he was incapable of holding the whole book in his head and his plot had gone straight off the tracks.

"Lu?"

Ian leaned back in his chair so that he could see into the kitchen.

Lucy's chair was empty, and her purple butterfly dress was hanging off the back of it. It hung neatly, as if she had taken it off before she shifted.

Ian swore under his breath and cheerfully called, "Lucy? Honey? Did you finish your food?" He should have kept her in a high chair a little longer, he thought woefully. But she was tall for her age and had convinced him that she was ready for a big girl chair. She was, but was he?

The sandwich that she'd been playing with had been disassembled and all the parts she liked had been eaten out. The halved cherry tomatoes were gone, of course, they never lasted long enough to be entertainment. Her sippy cup was on its side, a few drops of water on the table beneath it.

"Lucy, you know I don't want to play hide and seek right now. Lucy?"

Ian was equal parts annoyed and worried. There was so much trouble that a little girl could get into...and even more that a squirrel could. He'd barely looked away, and she'd been so safely occupied. He was the worst dad, he was a miserable failure, how hard could it be to juggle a stay-at-home career and one small child?

Pretty damned hard, it turned out. Ian scanned the top of the fridge and the cabinets in the kitchen; Lucy liked high places. But she wasn't in any of her usual spots, and Ian spread his search zone down the hall. "Lucy, please come out. Honey, are we playing a game? You know that Daddy needs to get his book finished, but if you want me to, I can read you one of *your* books. Lucy?"

The carpet gave a suspicious squelch, right in front of the bathroom and Ian flung the door open to find that there was water in a shallow pool all across the floor. "Argh!" He was wearing socks, and they were immediately soaked as he dashed across to the sink, where the tap was still running. There was a washcloth lying across the bottom of the bowl and when Ian pulled it out, the water in the bowl swiftly drained away. A few water-logged dolls sagged at the bottom.

"Lucy!!"

Ian made himself temper his voice. Lucy had probably realized that she'd done something wrong and was hiding as a squirrel in one of the million tiny places in this house that he'd never find her.

"Lucy, you aren't in trouble," he called as gently as he could. "I just need to know that you're okay!"

He pulled the towels down off the rack to start sopping up the puddle. He had a box fan somewhere, he'd better get it going in the hallway before they had a mold problem to add to the mix.

The phone rang while he was wringing out the towels the second time. "Hang on," he said when the fan drowned out the caller.

"You sound like you're in an air tunnel," Wanda complained when he got the fan turned off. When Ian was feeling his most lonely and full of regret over their broken relationship, she usually managed to say just the right thing to remind him why they'd parted ways.

"Sorry," he said, knowing he didn't sound sorry. "What's up?"

"I wanted to talk about The Schedule."

She always said it like both words were capitalized.

The Schedule.

The Schedule was the calendar that dictated the days they had to see each other, the days that Lucy was hers or his. At first, Wanda had been adamant about getting every day allotted to her with their joint custody, and Ian had spent the days she was gone desperately missing his daughter. But Wanda got busier with work, her new boyfriend had kids, and Wanda had gradually adjusted The Schedule so that Ian had Lucy nearly all the time. He'd even thought about pressuring her for child support, but it had never felt like it was worth the effort.

"After all," she'd said more than once. "You don't work, it's not an inconvenience to you."

Ian wasn't sure which part of the statement he objected to most. But like most battles with Wanda, it simply wasn't worth fighting anymore.

"What about it?" Ian sounded more surly than he meant. Was she going to want to talk to Lucy? Did he have to admit that he didn't know where she was and that she'd just flooded the bathroom?

Wanda sounded almost sweet. "I know I said I didn't want any of the holidays this year, but my parents invited us up to Helena for Labor Day. They'd like to see Lucy."

Ian remembered holidays with Wanda's folks. They were all squirrel shifters, and while he adored his daughter beyond reason, the ceaseless chattering and the way Wanda's family was always in constant motion had always left him feeling like he'd been in a room full of mental vampires after only a few minutes. Having to stay with them had been a kind of fine-tuned torture.

Labor Day. "Let me check my calendar."

Ian didn't really have to look at it. Aside from the looming red BOOK DUE entry on his calendar, it was just a trudging list of nothing. The closest he'd gotten to a social life lately was babysitting his friend Roderick's daughter Gabby, a little girl just younger than Lucy, while Roderick took his new girlfriend out on a date.

Sometimes, it seemed like everyone was moving on without him.

"That should work fine," Ian said.

"You're a peach," Wanda said sunnily. "I'll pick her up on Saturday morning and drop her off on Monday evening. Let me talk to Lucy."

Dammit.

"Hang on." He muted the phone, double-checking that he had, and then hollered, "Lucy! Come talk to your mom! She's on the phone *right now!*"

A rustle at the baseboard gave him a few seconds of warning, and then Lucy was shooting out from behind the heater, her rusty red fur covered in dust.

She flowed up into a little girl, completely naked, and reached grabby hands for the phone.

"I'll hold it for you, honey," Ian said, thumbing the connection back on. He knew there were parents that would casually hand children Lucy's age a several hundred dollar phone—Wanda among them—but he didn't trust her attention span and he couldn't afford to replace it.

"Mummy! Bathroom's all wet!"

Ian couldn't hear Wanda's answer to that, and he oversaw half of a halting conversation before Lucy agreed, "Kisses!" and waved at the phone.

Ian checked to see that Wanda had hung up and put the phone back in his pocket. "You want to tell me about the bathroom?" he asked.

Lucy eyed her escape route back under the heater and Ian made a note to try to block it up with something. His entire house had become an obstacle course of trying to keep her out of small places and dangerous things. The cabinet locks were a constant frustration, as much for him as they were for her, and she could climb *anything.*

"You're not in trouble," Ian promised. "I just want to make sure it doesn't happen again, honey."

She wilted and mumbled something about dolls, carrots, and possibly the Ukraine.

"Just make sure you ask me before you play in the bathroom," Ian begged. "And turn off the water. We don't want to waste it!"

Lucy looked up at him hopefully, then said, "I'm hungry."

It was her get-out-jail-free card. Ian wasn't going to deny her *food,* no matter how recently she'd eaten, and he bent and scooped her up into his arms. "What did you forget, sweety?"

Lucy put two fingers in her mouth and said, "clothes?" around them.

"Clothes," Ian agreed. "You're supposed to take your clothes with you when you shift."

Ian found himself at eye level with the business card that Roderick had given him the week before as he opened the fridge. Cherry's new day care for shifter children, Tiny Paws, apparently taught kids to shift with their clothing.

A day care for shifter children.

Maybe he could talk Wanda into helping to pay for it. Maybe, if he could finish his damned book, he could pay for it himself. It would be good for Lucy to get more socialization. He couldn't just go set up playdates with the neighborhood kids when she was so good at shifting and so terrible about knowing when she was supposed to.

"Do you want a yogurt squeezie?" Ian offered. He knew she would.

When he put her down for a protesting nap, an hour later, he went back to his laptop. There were sticky squirrel footprints on the lid.

I know how to fix this, he thought hopefully.

He opened up his phone and punched in the number for Tiny Paws.

"Hi," he said when Cherry answered. "I was wondering if you had any openings…"

Dragon's Instinct continues Ian and Lucy's story!